The Adventures of Jill's Ponies

By Jemma Spark

Book Nine of Jemma Spark's Jill Series

Epona Publishing

www.ponybookuniverse.com

Trade paperback ISBN 978-0-6450263-8-2

Jill Books

Jill Rides Cross Country (Jill Series Book 1)

Jill Has Two Horses (Jill Series Book 2)

Jill Goes Pony Trekking (Jill Series Book 3)

Jill and the Mystery of the Missing Horse (Jill Short Story)

Jill and the Steeplechaser (Jill Series Book 4)

Jill Dreams of a Dressage Horse (Jill Series Book 5)

Jill and the Horsemasters (Jill Series Book 6)

All Change at Blainstock Stables (Jill Series Book 7)

Jill's Ponies: Black Boy and Rapide (Jill Series Book 8)

The Adventures of Jill's Ponies (Jill Series Book 9)

Jill and the Prize Winners (Jill Series Book 10)

The Jill Crewe Miscellany No. One

Jill and the Wild Horses (Jill Series Book 11)

Table of Contents

Chapter One – Musical Horses

Susan King woke on Monday morning after the Blossom Park Hunter Trials and floated down to the kitchen to prepare her husband Barty's breakfast before he went off to work at a law firm in Rychester. He was his usual fussy, prim self, but this morning she merely smiled at him angelically, "Yes, Barty, no, Barty, anything you say, Barty."

"I hope you're not going over to your father's to ride that horse again today," he said peevishly.

Susan looked at him from beneath her lashes. She noticed how flat were his cheeks, how thin his lips and his eyes a cold-grey that gave nothing away, like the blank windows of a house which is unoccupied until suddenly a shrewd-looking person pops up behind the glass and shoots out a sharp little malevolent glance.

When he said, 'that horse', he was referring to Diablo, a bad-tempered coal-black gelding who jumped like a leaping machine but had a decidedly evil bent. At the weekend, Susan and Diablo had come a creditable fourth in the open event at Blossom Park. The year before, she had ridden him in the ladies' race at Grassmere Point-to-Point and come second to Jill Crewe on Black Comedy.

The fact that she had come second was not the issue. It was rather that Jill Crewe had beaten her. If it had been anyone else, it wouldn't have mattered. Susan, whose maiden name was Pyke, and Jill were adversaries from way back. They had grown up in the small village of Chatton in Oxfordshire and had been rivals throughout their childhoods. Jill had had two ponies Black Boy and Rapide, and she had looked after them herself, schooling and competing on them. Susan had been bought one fancy pony after another and had spent her time at school making snaky remarks about Jill, who had often returned this ill-feeling with sharp retorts.

But this morning, Susan was not concerned about Jill, who was far away at Porlock Vale, in Exmoor, working hard on becoming a qualified riding instructor.

"Of course not, darling," Susan purred in response to her husband's comment.

She had a quite different secret plan. She would take the train into Oxford and just happen to walk by Lonsdale College, hoping to catch a glimpse of Austin Pevensy, or perhaps, in the realms of a miracle, bump into him in the street. She had fallen hook, line and sinker (as the cliché goes) for Austin, one of the five Pevensy children of the Duke and Duchess of Tolkington. The story of her path to this infatuation is told in *Jill's Ponies: Black Boy and Rapide*, and now readers can follow in her footsteps as she pursues her obsession with this personable, young aristocratic man. She had become disillusioned with marriage to Bartholomew King, who she now considered the most uninspiring, petty, and unimaginative man in the whole of Oxfordshire.

After Barty had left for work, she dressed carefully for her expedition, pondering the sort of outfit that would make her look attractive to a young gentleman such as Austin. Perhaps he would admire a modern style, casual, certainly not gloves and a handbag on the arm like a middle-aged matron. After much deliberation, she selected a pair of casual slacks, brogue shoes and a bright red jumper with an elegant silk scarf tied around her neck. It was not bohemian but as young and casual as she could manage. Making a note to look at what other young women in Oxford were wearing, she decided that clothes shopping was her next mission. But certainly, not from Creations, the upmarket Oxford boutique that was favoured by middle-class matrons where she had recently worked for one horrendous day before making excuses and never returning.

Stepping off the train in Oxford, she realised that she had no idea where Lonsdale College was situated. She had lived in Chatton all her life and regularly gone to Oxford on shopping expeditions but knew nothing about the colleges that were dotted around the city. Walking down the high street looking into shop windows, she thought she might have to buy a tourist guidebook when, by the greatest good luck, or perhaps ordained by Fate who was smiling upon her, she bumped into Aggie, none other than the Duchess of Tolkington and Austin's mother.

"Oh! Duchess!" cried Susan, blushing bright red as if caught in a shameful act, not merely walking down a street.

"Oh, it's Susan, Susan King," said Aggie, who always remembered names as social connections were her business. "For heaven's sake, don't call me Duchess. I'm Aggie to everyone. You're Evelyn's god daughter, I believe. I don't know why we haven't met before. That was a good effort you made at Blossom Park, and that black horse doesn't look like an easy ride."

It was the first time Susan had ever spoken to Aggie, and she was amazed that a Duchess came across as such a girlish creature, with bright, lively eyes and the voice of a young woman. Perhaps it was horses that kept you young, for, by all accounts, Aggie was as horse-mad as any teenage girl.

"I was rather pleased, but it was your daughter Porsche who was the heroine of the hour," replied Susan in a fawning tone. "To win both the novice horse and open event was a miraculous achievement. She is such an amazing horsewoman!"

"Yes, she did well. And she hadn't been riding that horse for long. He was just off the track and not looking at all promising," said Aggie.

In truth, Porsche had been given the horse, Mangala, to ride as a punishment after she had carelessly ridden her older sister's Mercedes' star mount, Banjo and staked him on the wing of a water jump, resulting in him being put down. Porsche had turned the tables on everyone, and without the systematic groundwork needed for training a horse, which she considered unnecessary for such a rider as herself, she had ridden Mangala with sheer determination and had beaten all the competition.

Now, Porsche had been promised another horse of her own, as she was never to ride Mercedes' horses again, and Aggie was interested in Diablo. His lack of goodwill and kindness seemed a good match for Porsche, who could be described as a 'difficult character'.

"Have you had that black horse long?" asked Aggie artlessly.

"Well, he's not mine. He's my father's horse," replied Susan.

"Perhaps you should get something a little easier to ride," suggested Aggie confidingly. "I'm not saying you're not up to it, but it can't be much fun for you."

Susan looked at her. How very astute this woman was! She didn't like riding Diablo at all, he was such an unkind brute, and her father certainly avoided getting on him.

In her turn, Aggie was looking consideringly at Susan. She might just be a suitable friend for Porsche, who never invited anyone to the house. Aggie wasn't even sure who were Porsche's friends. Sometimes she wondered if Porsche had friends at all, but her school mistress had declaimed her as the 'leader of the pack'. She had seen Susan bonding with Austin and Porsche when she had sat with them during the Blossom Park prize-giving. Perhaps she might be a good influence on Porsche whose disposition was, to say the very least troublesome.

"You must come to dinner at Pevensy Park," said Aggie. "Come early, and I can show you some of the horses that we're thinking of selling. We won't be asking a fortune for them, just looking for good homes. I seem to have accumulated far too many horses, again." She made it sound like a regular occurrence.

"Oh! I would love it," gushed Susan.

"Next Saturday night, there's some friends of Mercedes coming, the Wootton-Smiths, and of course Austin will be back from college. It should be a jolly young crowd. Come at three, and we can go for a ride. I'll look at the horses and see if there's something you might particularly like. I'm sure we can have a jolly time discussing the merits of each of them," said Aggie.

She took a step to continue on her way, but as an afterthought, turned back.

"We do dress for dinner, so come in your riding clothes and bring something suitable for the evening."

Susan floated away. She would have to find an evening dress that was suitable for dining at the table of the local aristocrats. An outfit that would cast a spell over Austin so he would never look at another woman. It was quite thirty minutes before she remembered that she was married. Aggie had assumed that she was single. Thus, the invitation hadn't included Barty. It could be awkward to attend a dinner party without one's husband, but Susan had no intention of taking him along. It would inevitably come to light that she was married, and it would look odd that she hadn't mentioned him before, but that could be dealt with later. At this moment, nothing mattered except this precious invitation that had been dropped from the heavens upon her head. It was her entrée into the magic circle that she had longed for. The last person she wanted to come along was boring old Barty!

If only Barty could drop dead of a heart attack! Of course, she would have to go through the motions of a grieving widow, but Austin could console her, and within months they would be together. Such a vision of pure bliss lit up her face and clasping her hands together; she looked to the heavens.

Ducking down into some of the Oxford side streets, she looked for suitable boutiques. Groovy boutiques, that was what Ann Derry would call them. Ann had been in her form at school, certainly not one of her own group but the best friend of Jill Crewe.

Susan rifled through the racks of clothes in various shops but could find nothing that appealed to her in any way and certainly nothing she would dream of wearing. In the end, she went into the news agency and bought some fashion magazines. It was only Monday. She would bone up on the latest styles and perhaps dash into London to shop there. Carnaby Street! Maybe that would be the place to go.

Aggie went home and began to plot her latest social gathering. Young people that was the thing. Like-minded horsey people who could be chums with Porsche and help steer her into more tranquil waters. Then, she remembered Henry Thurston, the local vet, who was going out with Ann Derry. Ann was a bright young woman, indelibly horsey, fun and witty.

That would be just the thing. Aggie had no idea of the long history of tension between Susan and Ann. She began to consider numbers. There was that couple that Mercedes had invited who were interested in buying another horse. She totted up the other guests, Mercedes, Porsche, Susan and Ann and then Royce, Austin, and Henry, and she needed one other man to balance the numbers. She racked her brain. She would send a note to Austin and tell him to bring one of his jolly young friends home for the weekend. But, then, knowing Austin's gregarious nature, he was sure to turn up with a troop of young people. Cook would have to be warned to have extra supplies to hand in case the catering numbers went up at short notice. They would use the large dining room, so it was merely a matter of setting extra places.

She dashed off a note inviting Ann and Henry to dinner and addressed the envelope to Pool Cottage. Although Ann's parents still lived in Chatton, Ann had moved into Jill's childhood home and had the use of the two stables and a field with an orchard. The cottage had two bedrooms, and when Jill visited Chatton she had somewhere to stay.

Aggie also wrote a note to Austin at Lonsdale telling him to bring home one of his nice young gentlemen friends. She went to the kitchen and told Cook what she was planning and asked her to come up with a menu and then hurried down to the stables. This was a far more important mission. She needed to do a stock take of the Pevensy horses and decide which they could bear to part with. She called Bert Munro, the stable manager, into the office and together, they looked through the records.

"I need a list of every horse over the age of three, broken or unbroken, and what stage of training he or she is at. I've promised Louis that we're going to get organised and trim our numbers and make sure there's nothing promising skulking in a back field and not being ridden. Can you mark with an asterisk anything that you think might be suitable for Porsche? I want her to have something decent to work with now she's proved herself with Mangala."

Aggie liked to cover all the bases, in case Diablo wasn't suitable, or Susan's father wasn't willing to sell him. Bert nodded his head wisely. He was an inveterate record-keeper, and it would only take an hour or so to get such a list together.

"By the way, how did Mangala pull up on Sunday morning?" she asked.

"He's still green, in both senses," he replied wryly, "but he's trotting out sound, although he looks a bit hollow. I'll be keeping my eye on him for the next few days. He certainly got ridden hard."

There was a faint note of censure in his voice, but he had been working for Aggie for a long time, and he was a master of circumspection. He knew that Porsche was a sensitive subject, and he didn't want to rock the boat. On the morning of the hunter trials, they discovered that someone had got into Mangala's loose box and coloured him bright, iridescent green with food dye. Obviously, Porsche had upset someone. She had not only won both events but on a bright green horse.

"Can you clip Mangala and see if you can't get most of that green off him? Then, of course, he'll need to be double rugged if he goes out and an extra blanket at night. The sooner we can get rid of the Green Flash, the better," said Aggie. "Thank goodness there was no photographer from *Horse and Hound* there at the weekend."

"Very well, madame," said Bert.

Mercedes was in the yard getting Tom, one of the grooms, to trot up Sirius and Sassy Swoop to make sure they had suffered no ill-effects after their exertions at the hunter trials. Aggie told her of the plan to shed some horses. She looked thoughtful.

"Mummy, I was thinking. I do love Sassy with her mischievous spirit, but I have to face the fact that she is not really going to make it to the top. For a start, she's a mare, and they can be so unreliable in big competitions, perhaps she might be happier in a home where she can go hacking, jump in local events and be petted and adored and the indisputable star of the show."

"Oh, Mercedes! My dear girl, you're so *sensible*!" said Aggie smiling proudly at her favourite daughter. "I think you're right now that you've said it. With all this myriad of horses, there still isn't anything that has the promise of Banjo. I think we might have to go shopping, perhaps in Europe, and find you something really top-notch. To do that, we must do a cull to persuade Louis that it's a good idea."

"Mummy, you know you can persuade Daddy just by batting your eyelashes," laughed Mercedes. "I only hope when I get saddled with a husband I can manage him so effectively!"

"Do you think your friends, the Wootton-Smiths that you've invited this weekend, might be interested in her?"

"Absolutely not. They want something sensible. In fact, Sirius would be right up their street, come to think of it. Sirius would be made-to-measure."

"You're thinking of getting rid of your *two* horses who are already competing!" exclaimed Aggie.

"If I'm serious about eventing, then I have to make hard decisions and finding the right horse is a big part of it. Otherwise, all the training in the world isn't going to turn them into a champion," said Mercedes.

"I wonder if Susan King might be interested in Sassy. She's obviously more of a casual competitor, and you can tell that underneath, she's scared stiff of Diablo, but she can't be such a bad rider to have got him around that course clear at the weekend. Sassy might be just the thing for her," said Aggie thoughtfully.

"Well, Sassy has certainly got the looks and the glamour, and for all her naughtiness, she has a sweet nature and is only mischievous, not devilish," said Mercedes.

"We'll put Susan on her at the weekend and see how they get on," said Aggie. "And if you can bear it, offer Sirius to the Wootton-Smiths, and then we'll find you some horses that will take you right to the top!"

Chapter Two – An Unlikely Alliance

When Aggie's invitation popped onto the mat at Pool Cottage, Ann swooped it up with delight.

"Just look at this!" she exclaimed aloud, talking to herself. "An invitation to Saturday night dinner at Pevensy Park. Gosh! Henry and I are moving up the social ladder! I simply must go to London and buy myself a new outfit!"

Thus, it was by another of those coincidences that often pop up in the lives of young people, especially those who are written about in books such as this, that Ann and Susan were both travelling on the same train to London. They were sitting at either end of the carriage, and Ann was determined that it would be just too weird for them not to chat. She tripped down the aisle, slid over sat beside Susan and began to tell her about her Saturday night invitation.

Susan was surprised. Somehow, she had thought that her new world that was centred on the Pevensys was in quite a different league to her previous humdrum Chatton life. She was rather put out. But as Ann continued in her friendly way confessing that she was off to buy herself an outfit, Susan admitted that she too was invited and intended to find herself something rather swish.

"Do you think it is black tie?" asked Ann. "I don't remember reading it on the invitation, but I'll have to check and make sure that Henry has got his kit dry-cleaned and ready to go."

"I don't know," said Susan. "I wasn't sent a formal invitation, I just ran into Aggie yesterday in Oxford, and she invited me."

There was that knotty problem. Of course, Ann would assume that Barty was accompanying her. But for the time being, Susan decided to remain mum on the subject. It would wreck everything if Barty had to come as well, and it was worth pretending that married women were invited to attend dinner parties without their husbands every day of the week. If it came to it, she could claim she was too embarrassed to mention it to Aggie at the time of the invitation and had decided it was better to go without him.

The train steamed into King's Cross. Susan followed in Ann's wake, jumping onto a bus and climbing the stairs to the top deck to enjoy a grand view, looking out at the sights as they trundled down to Chelsea. Susan was rather intrigued to find that Ann knew her way around this neck of the woods. It seems that she was an *habituée* of some of the grooviest boutiques in Kings Road.

"Tartine said she could meet me for coffee at eleven, and then she's going to help me choose something. She's French, you know, Parisian and has impeccable taste when it comes to clothes," said Ann.

Susan hated to admit it, but this was a godsend. If she were to aspire to become a jazzy young woman of the sixties, she was going to need some guidance. To her surprise, she was finding that Ann without Jill was delightful company. She smiled to herself to imagine what Jill would think if she managed to appropriate her best friend. How her world was suddenly turned upside down!

They met Tartine in a crowded coffee shop that appeared to be the meeting place of every bright young London person that morning. Susan was bowled over by the sheer elegance of Ann's friend: her divine French accent, her clothes that looked like she had stepped straight out of the pages of Vogue, her sophisticated manner and pretty, vivacious face with a different expression every few seconds.

This exotic creature began to tell them a story about a girl she knew, who had been to one of *those* parties where Christine Keeler was often a guest. Susan didn't dare ask who exactly was Christine Keeler. She could vaguely remember something about Profumo and a Russian spy. Not wanting to show her ignorance, she ooh-ed and aah-ed in time with Ann's reactions, resolving to find out as soon as possible what it was all about. Feeling like a country bumpkin who knew nothing about the latest scandals in London, she resolved that things were going to change!

After coffee and at least two delicious pastries each, they followed Tartine to various boutiques. She seemed to know every proprietor and sales assistant and imperiously decided just which outfits they should wear. Her taste was absolutely bang on. Susan looked at herself in the shop mirror and saw an elegant stranger in the most divine dress, a silver sheath that finished above her knees with an intricate pattern of coloured sequins and subtle embroidery. The price tag was astronomical, but she happily wrote out a cheque. Barty would just have to swallow it down and suppress his lower-middle-class frugal tendencies. He had wanted a beautiful wife, and now he had one, and she needed to be dressed accordingly. Ann was tending more to a bohemian look. With her cap of bright-red hair, she was naturally flamboyant. With the help of Tartine, she chose a bright blue peasant-gypsy dress with tiny mirrors sewn into it and lavish yellow and red ribbons swirling around the hem.

"All I need now are the castanets," she cried, twirling around in front of the mirror.

Then the three of them proceeded to a shoe shop and chose high-heeled silver shoes for Susan and a pair of bright red dancing shoes for Ann.

"You two will be the *belles* of the ball, the peak of the mode," said Tartine, misunderstanding that it was merely a dinner party for country people who rode horses.

"Oh, Henry will adore this outfit!" said Ann. She knew, of course, that Henry adored her whether she was wearing the most modish of outfits or a coal sack. He took delight in her exuberance and vivacity.

"I must go," said Tartine, "I have a lunch appointment. It was very nice to meet you Suzanne." She whisked away and left Ann and Susan clutching their shopping bags on the pavement.

"Let's go to a matinée," said Ann. "It's a shame to waste a day in London. We can head up to Leicester Square and see what is on. Sometimes you can get half-price tickets just before the show begins."

Susan could think of no reason not to, and they leapt on a bus. They saw a delightful comedy, and Susan found herself laughing right through it. Unwittingly she seemed to have discovered life as she had dreamed it might be lived and with Ann Derry of all people!

They had a glass of wine at the bar of the Dorchester hotel before they caught the train back to Oxford. Susan felt an almost irrepressible desire to pour out her heart to Ann and tell her about Barty and her horrid married life and how she had fallen in love with Austin. But she was not quite so far gone to make this foolish move. It was something she had to keep hidden in her heart for now.

She got home only half an hour before Barty was due to step through the door. Instinctively she hid her purchases in the back of the cupboard under the stairs. She cleaned her teeth, so her breath didn't smell of wine and threw together dinner. Frying sausages and onions, boiling potatoes and stirring gravy, she managed to land this simple supper on the table in a timely manner, and Barty had no cause for comment.

The next few days were tortuous. She went to see her father and rode Diablo for him.

"Daddy, do you think we could sell him? You don't really like riding him yourself, and he's no fun at all," she said.

"But he's a magnificent beast. Everyone admires his looks!" said George Pyke.

"But they don't have to ride him!" she cried. "Aggie Pevensy said she might have something for me that would be more of a suitable ladies' ride."

"I can't see that Barty wanting to shell out on the purchase of another horse for you," said George, who might be big and bluff but not totally without insight into the character of his son-in-law.

"Oh Daddy, would you buy another horse for me?" she asked, turning to him with a winsome appealing expression that she knew would always twist his heart with love.

"Humph," he replied.

There was still the issue of escaping on Saturday afternoon and not returning until late at night. Susan couldn't bear the thought of telling Barty where she was going. He would be outraged that he was not invited. He would think that dinner at the Pevensys might be a chance for him to impress some important people who would bring business into the firm.

Then by a miracle, brought about by Barty and his family's nasty, small-minded natures, his mother rang him on Friday night. It seemed that they had people staying for the weekend, but one of his father's golf friends had dropped out of the game on Sunday. She asked Barty to come for the weekend and fill in the gap. Unfortunately, the house was full to the gunnels, and he would have to sleep on the put-me-up in the study, and there would be no room for Susan.

Barty announced the arrangement with a sly grin.

"You were away last weekend, off gallivanting on that horse, so this weekend it's my turn for some fun," he declared.

Susan's heart filled to bursting with joy at this announcement. What a stroke of luck! Fate was working with her! She was sure that her romance with Austin was written in the stars! She looked down at her lap and tried to appear apologetic.

"Barty, I'm happy for you to have this chance, and you're quite right. You deserve some fun," she said meekly.

He smiled at her in triumph, feeling as if he had won this domestic battle. Susan's horsey tendencies needed to be curbed, and this would teach her a lesson!

Like a faithful subservient wife who knew her place, she waved Barty off at eleven o'clock on Saturday morning, after cooking him his favourite bacon and eggs with mushrooms and tomatoes, but no fried bread – that was too extravagant for him. She had dressed in a sensible housewifely skirt and blouse with a pinafore over the top. She had told Barty, and he believed her, that she would spend the weekend giving their home an extra special cleaning.

As soon as he drove off, she dived into the cupboard beneath the stairs and retrieved her hidden shopping bags. She needed to try on that evening dress again. She was worried that she had been carried away and had chosen something that was just not right. She slithered into it and slipped her feet into the silver shoes.

Truly a Cinderella moment! Turning this way and that in front of the mirror, she almost didn't recognise herself. She kept an eye out the window in case Barty returned home, having forgotten something. Feeling deliciously guilty about her visit to the Pevensys, she wondered if the house would whisper her secret to Barty. She sometimes feared that the very walls were in league with him to entrap her into the most humdrum existence.

Taking off the silver dress and carefully packing a case with her best silk underwear which had been purchased for her honeymoon, she added her only genuine pearl necklace and her mother's white stole to wrap around her shoulders, just in case she and Austin slipped out into the garden for a moment alone. Then she laid out her best riding clothes and got dressed. She was ready far too early and felt too churned up inside to eat lunch. It didn't occur to her to do even a scrap of housework.

The minutes dragged by, and eventually, it was time to leave. She climbed into her little car and tootled down the road, humming to herself. She almost felt as if she were running away to a new life and would never have to return to dull old Rychester.

Chapter Three – Pevensys' Horse Paradise

Susan had never been to Pevensy Park before. She drove through the village of Langton Shrove, a scattering of cottages, a tiny, abandoned church and a phone box. Probably the village belonged to the Pevensys, she thought. What must it be like to own a whole village? Further on, she came to the estate's impressively grand gates, with carved gryphons sitting atop ornate pillars. The statues represented mythical creatures, a formidable combination of lion and eagle, which surveyed the countryside and protected the estate from enemies.

A tiny cottage that must have once been the gatekeeper's lodge was at the entrance and beyond a magnificent park. A huge expanse of perfectly tended green grass dotted with large skeletons of oak trees spreading their branches. The road curved to the left and right, and then in the distance, she could see the large house. It was huge, big enough for more than ten families.

"Imagine the cleaning!" thought Susan, who had recently grappled with the issue of house cleaning and supervising a woman who came in twice a week. You would need an army of servants to keep that place scrubbed and dusted.

She drove up the front drive and parked off to the side. Tentatively she climbed out of her car and approached the steps up to the magnificent front door. She rang the bell and waited, feeling unaccountably nervous. Perhaps she had misunderstood, even imagined her encounter with Aggie in Oxford, dreamed up the invitation. No-one appeared. She wondered if she should ring the bell again. She was on the point of turning around, leaping back in the car and driving away.

"Oh! Hello!" called a light musical voice.

Susan spun around. It was Mercedes.

"Good afternoon," she stuttered nervously. "Aggie said I should come and see some horses."

"You must be Susan King," said Mercedes. "Do come over to the stables. I have some friends there, and we're going to be riding this afternoon. Mummy has had a most marvellous idea for a horse for you."

Mercedes led the way, striding with long graceful steps, around the side of the house and through a tunnel of shrubbery. Despite herself, Susan was overawed at the sight of the magnificent stable yard.

"Mummy, Susan is here. I found her on the doorstep," called Mercedes.

Susan had a ridiculous flashing image of herself in a cardboard box, left like an unwanted baby on the steps of a rich family's house.

"Let me introduce you to Rosemary and Bruce Wootton-Smith. They're here to look at horses as well," said Mercedes.

They all chorused 'how do you do' and looked each other over in a polite manner. The Wootton-Smiths could have been brother and sister. Both had pale brown hair, white skin and similar nondescript features. Susan wondered if they were siblings or a married couple.

"We're all here now," said Aggie, emerging from the office where she had been in conference with Bert Munro. "Tom has a collection of horses saddled up for us, and I thought we could ride around the park and pop over a few jumps. Susan, we have a rather special mare for you. You would have seen Mercedes riding her at Blossom Park." Tom led forward the gorgeous grey mare. "This is Sassy Swoop."

Susan was astonished.

"But she's one of Mercedes' competition horses!"

"Yes, she is. But Mercedes has decided she might not ever make it to Burghley or Badminton. We think she might do better at the local competition level, hacking out, perhaps even having some gorgeous foals. You know if you put her to an Arab or Anglo-Arab stallion, the progeny would be divinely pretty!"

It crossed Susan's mind that she was listening to a sales spiel. Surely the Pevensys were not so desperate to offload their horses that they had to do the hard sell on their friends and acquaintances.

"For you, Bruce, dear, there is Sirius. He's another one that Mercedes has been training, but again we're not sure that he is quite up to Burghley or Badminton standard. He's an absolute dear. You could trust a child on his back, and he'd make sure he took them out in total safety and security, but he's got quite a jump in him. Like Sassy, he went clear around the open course at Blossom Park Hunter Trials, but they didn't have the fastest times. Rosemary, I've put you on Troubadour. He's such a reliable old darling. Of course, we'd never part with him, but he is a lovely ride."

Perhaps Rosemary was not much of a rider, so she was being given a faithful, old dobbin, thought Susan.

Aggie mounted Austin's Firefly. He was prancing around, refusing to stand still. She pursed her lips. You could see she was thinking that Austin was letting this horse get away with anything. Mercedes was riding a young, ex-racehorse that she was training. Porsche suddenly rushed into the yard and shouted imperiously to Tom that he should saddle Mangala for her.

"Hello, Susan," she said, ignoring the Wootton-Smiths, her mother and her sister.

"Hi, Porsche," said Susan, startled that she had been singled out. She had a sneaking fear of Porsche, which was wrapped up in slavish devotion to such a talented and determined young woman, not to mention the favourite sister of the divine Austin.

They clattered out of the stable yard in a cavalcade, then headed along the track that circumnavigated the park. Susan liked Sassy. The mare might be reputed to be mischievous, but she felt only good will exuding from her, very different to the black brutish vibes that emanated from Diablo.

"Trot on," called Aggie at the head of the line. Like a riding school, they obediently trotted on. Sirius bent his head correctly despite Bruce's fumbling hands. Troubadour seemed to respond to Aggie's voice command rather than Rosemary's inept leg aid. Mercedes' young horse threw his head in the air and tried to barge to the front, but she expertly held him back and persuaded him to proceed at an acceptable pace. Mangala was leaping about, but Porsche's firm seat and strong legs held him back, and he gave in and did what he was told. Sassy sprang into a lovely springy trot, flinging her feet out in front of her like a ballerina.

"Canter on," commanded Aggie from the front. The horses cantered.

"Over the log," called Aggie, and they proceeded towards a large tree branch that had been shorn of all twigs, making an ideal two-foot-six-inch jump. Sassy sprang forward eagerly, and Susan felt her leap beneath her, clearing it by at least a foot.

"She jumps well," said Susan to Porsche, who was riding beside her.

"Yes, she's a good mare," Porsche agreed. "But Mercedes only wants to compete on geldings. I think that's why they're looking for a new home for her."

They cantered on side by side.

"I liked that black horse that you rode last week," said Porsche casually. "Does he belong to you?"

"No, he's my father's. He bought him as a hunter, but he's a bit strong across country. Doesn't let him relax and chat to his cronies as they go. Truth be told I'm not sure that he really every rode him."

"I would love to have him as my own," said Porsche.

"Your mother was asking about him, too," said Susan. Then it came to her. This whole set-up. It was to get their hands on Diablo, and she was being offered Sassy in exchange. This family had to be admired for their aptitude for getting what they wanted. They went about it with such charm and persuasive good manners. Even Porsche could play that game when she wanted something. Susan smiled to herself. She wanted something too. She wanted Austin, and if a bit of horse dealing was part of the game, then she was happy to go along with it.

Susan wasn't upset to think that the Pevensys didn't really care about her. They probably didn't care about anyone else either. Obviously, they were interested in Diablo. Every relationship in life is a social exchange - she had read that cynical statement somewhere. Certainly not in one of Jill's books!

They were cantering towards a set of wooden post-and-rails, and she decided to aim for the highest level. Sassy was such fun to ride. She wondered whether her father would agree to exchange her for the black brute. Probably. If she begged him in her little-girl-pleading way, he had never really been able to resist her. She would play along with the Pevensys. This was all going to be rather fun. Tonight, Austin would be at dinner, and she would see him again.

They continued around the park, and now it was Aggie taking some time to slather on another layer of charm, like icing on a pink and white cake.

"You ride very well, Susan," she said graciously.

"That's very kind. Of course, I'm nowhere in Mercedes' and Porsche's league," admitted Susan.

"Porsche is very competitive," sighed Aggie.

"She did so well at the hunter trials. You must have been very proud of her," said Susan. She was longing to ask about the green dye but couldn't think of a way to introduce the subject. Besides, bringing up an uncomfortable topic might spoil the ambience of mutual admiration that was being carefully cultivated.

They got back to the stables, dismounted, and walked off, leaving the staff to deal with the horses. This is the way it should always be, thought Susan. Drifting through life, enjoying oneself and leaving the slog to other people. If she were with Austin, then she could enjoy life like this forever.

Aggie led the way down through the shrubbery tunnel, and they went inside for afternoon tea. There were two teapots, one with China tea, the other Earl Grey. Platters of thinly sliced bread and butter spread with a choice of Gentleman's Relish or salmon paste and slices of seed cake. All rather delicious. Susan had hardly been able to eat all week, with the excitement of her newly discovered infatuation, but now her appetite returned.

"Mercedes, darling, would you mind taking Susan upstairs so that she can rest and change for dinner," said Aggie.

"Of course, Mummy," said her eldest daughter.

Susan tripped up the stairs behind Mercedes. They walked along several long corridors until they reached Mercedes' bedroom. It was very large, painted a cheerful daffodil-yellow with three long windows that looked down over the fields. Mercedes went across and drew the curtains and put a match to the fire that was ready laid in the fireplace. Susan watched her with interest.

"Would you like a bath before you change for dinner?" Mercedes asked.

"Yes, that would be delightful," said Susan. "I've brought my dress. I left it in the car."

"That's no problem. I'll ring for someone to go down and get it."

Oh, to have servants at your beck and call every minute of the day, thought Susan longingly.

She went into the bathroom, and the bathtub was soon full of warm water. She sprinkled in some smelly stuff. Absolute heaven! Wallowing sensuously, she dreamed of Austin bursting through the door and kneeling beside the bath, declaring his love. It seemed like anything was possible in this magical place.

Wrapping herself in a fluffy pink bathrobe hanging on the back of the door, she wafted back down the corridor to Mercedes' room. Her dress and shoes were laid out on the bed, and Mercedes was writing at a small bureau desk.

Susan wasn't sure what to talk about. She was longing to find out about Austin, his character, his little habits, and his favourite things. But delightful as Mercedes was, she did not invite confidences. She held herself a little apart. There was something unapproachable and remote about her — the cool, untouchable princess.

Susan slipped into her dress and brushed her blonde curls until they shone. Then she looked in the long mirror and discreetly applied a little makeup, just a touch of blusher, a pale lipstick and a swipe of blue eyeshadow. She looked down at her hands, wincing just a little at the fact that she had deliberately left her wedding ring at home.

"Oh! You look divine in that dress," said Mercedes. "I suppose I had better change for dinner now."

They were ready to go downstairs when Porsche slunk down the hallway towards them, wearing a long black dress. Susan's mother would never have allowed her to wear black. She considered it immoral. Obviously, Aggie was more liberal in her ideas of colour schemes.

"Susan, come into my room. I just want to show you something," said Porsche. "You go on down, Mercedes. We'll follow you in a minute."

Susan was intrigued.

"What is it?" she asked curiously.

As Mercedes' room had been all light and good taste and big windows, Porsche's was like a cave. Posters of horses were plastered everywhere over dark-coloured walls.

"It's about Diablo. I'm serious. I want that horse."

"Oh," said Susan. "Well, certainly I can ask my father. I don't enjoy jumping him much, but I guess you could manage and get the most out of him."

"Can we go over and see your father tomorrow? Perhaps I can help you persuade him?"

Susan considered this proposition. She wasn't sure that her father would be up to dealing with the dark and dangerous Porsche. Then, inspiration came to her.

"My father is probably better at dealing with men. Do you think Austin could come with us? He might be more likely to persuade my father. You know, man to man."

"Of course, Austin will come along. I want to ride that black horse and feel how he goes, but I'm sure I can do something with him. If you stay the night, then we can drive over in the morning. Will your father be home?"

"Yes, if we go early. He usually pops down to the pub for a drink before a traditional Sunday lunch."

"I'll get someone to make up a bed for you in the guest wing," said Porsche. Instantly, Susan had visions of Austin tip-toeing along the corridors to come and see her in the middle of the night. Oh! If only!

They made their way down to the drawing room where Louis was serving pre-dinner drinks.

"A gin and tonic," said Susan, trying to be grown up and adopting her mother's favourite tipple.

"Oh, Susan, how lovely to see you," called Ann, who was standing next to Henry, chatting to the Wootton-Smiths. "Come and join us. Rosemary and Bruce have been telling us about their delightful ride this afternoon. I hear that you were on Sassy Swoop. Isn't that just the most gorgeous name for any horse!"

"Ann, I should have invited you to join us," said Aggie, with a gleam in her eye. "We've got some lovely young horses that are desperate for good homes. I hear that you're retiring that steeplechaser of yours. Perhaps you'd like to bring on a new horse for Henry to jump race."

"Well, that's certainly an idea," said Ann. "I've got Black Comedy and the little Totty, who was Mrs Darcy's faithful riding school pony, now retired in the field at Pool Cottage. It's starting to look like an old horse and pony shelter. When I go over to Bristol, we're going to have to find good homes for them. I was thinking the Miss Farthingtons might take them in. I hear they have quite a menagerie over there."

At this comment, Mercedes looked interested.

"I liked that skewbald horse that that riding school instructor rode at the hunter trials. Do you know what they're going to do with that one?" she asked.

"I have no idea," said Ann brightly. "I guess Serena might jump him in local competitions and go from there. It's a brilliant chance for her. Wendy Mead has got her young gelding to bring on, and now Serena's got a competition prospect."

Susan hoped that this might put off Mercedes, so she wouldn't think of purloining Patchwork, just when it looked like Serena was getting her big chance.

"Austin hasn't arrived yet with his college chums," said Aggie to the room at large. "He's always late, the naughty boy."

Susan had butterflies in her tummy. She cast constant glances towards the door, waiting for the golden boy to make his entrance. Then the door opened and in came a bevy of handsome young people, not just young men but a couple of girls as well.

"Oh! Austin! My darling! As ever, you make an entrance," said Aggie, counting at least six heads. Thank goodness she had told Cook to prepare extra.

Susan felt as insignificant as a small insect, standing at the side of the room looking at this bunch of happy-go-lucky young people who exuded self-confidence and social joyfulness. Sharp-eyed, she looked over the girls. They were both tiny, gamine, like waifs with their eyes ringed by black kohl, short, carelessly tousled hair, and clothes that might have been picked up in a jumble sale but worn with such style and panache that they looked like they could go tripping down a catwalk. Susan was floored. For all her careful dressing, artfully applied make-up and matching shoes, she could never carry it off like these girls. She felt like a dowdy shop mannequin in a department store.

"Let's go into dinner, darlings," called Aggie. "Austin, you and your chums can forego pre-prandial drinks."

"That's alright, Mamma," said Austin cheerfully. "I must admit we did stop at a pub on the way."

"Of course, you did," said Louis, with a hint of censure, but even he couldn't carry it off in the face of the cheerful hilarity that swirled around this bunch of bright young things.

They passed by the small dining room. Susan glimpsed the polished wood walls, the fancy plastered ceiling and the paintings that made it look like an art gallery. Tonight, they were in the long formal dining room that must have been used for state dinners with politicians and royalty in a bygone age. The walls were wallpapered with a warm coral colour patterned with swirls and rosettes that were artfully tinted with an aqua-marine colour. The high ceiling arched over them, painted with the same aqua colour. There were no paintings or animal heads on the walls, and this lack of traditional decoration worked very well. A crisp, white damask cloth was draped over the table, and each setting was perfect as if a ruler had been used to measure the exact distance between the cutlery and the edge of the table.

Susan found herself between two of Austin's friends, with Porsche across the table and one of the chic young women. It was gratifying that she was considered one of the college people and not down the end of the table with Mercedes and the dull old Wootton-Smiths. Ann and Henry were a little further along, positioned mid-way between the young people and the more staid and respectable ones.

Susan surreptitiously observed Ann in this social setting. She had certainly come on since their school days. When she moved and smiled, everyone around her relaxed. Her eyes sparkled, and although she wasn't classically beautiful like Mercedes or Porsche, there was a kind of glowing halo sitting upon her head, which was perhaps something to do with her cap of unfashionably bright red hair.

Austin was sitting further down the table and Susan couldn't quite hear what he was saying. There was an elaborate candelabra blocking her view of his face. He was laughing with one of the waif-girls, and she feared that this was probably his current girlfriend. The bottom dropped out of her dreams, which now seemed ridiculous. Austin was so far out of her league that she couldn't imagine how she had thought he might be interested in her. Thank goodness she had confided in no one! This was a major consolation. In time, she would persuade herself that it had been merely a passing attraction. The important thing was that she was now on the fringes of the Pevensys' social circle. Although once they got their hands on Diablo, she might be dropped like a hot potato.

Dinner passed in a whirl of five courses (no less!), and Susan was determined to eat as if to prove to herself that last week's loss of appetite had been merely an aberration. It didn't even matter if the fact that she was married came to light. It was a bulwark against imagined humiliation. Undoubtedly, her father would mention Barty tomorrow in front of Porsche and Austin. She would carry it off without a qualm. Then tomorrow night, she would tell Barty all about her weekend, and it would be tit-for-tat with his smug assumption that she had missed out on what would surely have been a deadly weekend with his ghastly parents.

Chapter Four – Dastardly Diablo

Susan was ensconced in a very comfortable guest bedroom, along a passageway in one of the wings. The waif-girls were a few doors away. All the young people that Austin had brought were staying over after a night of such freely flowing wine that it would have been impossible for them to venture out onto the road. Susan found a new toothbrush, a tube of toothpaste, and a comb neatly placed on the shelf beside the washbasin in her room. It was part of the course for guests to stay the night without prior arrangements.

She lay for a while staring up at the ceiling, thinking how pleasant it was to sleep alone without her husband. She dared not even drift into any sort of idea about lying there with Austin, that would have been ridiculous, and the sooner she banished such thoughts from her mind, the better. Tomorrow, she was to take Porsche, and perhaps Austin, to visit her father. She had always been proud of her father, and her family's large house, certainly bigger than Pool Cottage, but compared to Pevensy Park, it was a hovel. She would have to hold her head high and carry it off with aplomb.

In the morning, over a sumptuous breakfast, it was decided that Aggie should accompany them to see Diablo and do the negotiations rather than Austin. Susan was relieved. The excursion would be about Diablo and persuading her father to part with him. She rang ahead, so they didn't just turn up and warned him of the purpose of the visit. He sounded surprised but not annoyed. Good old Daddy, she had always been able to rely on him.

Porsche was dressed in her riding clothes and looking more determined than ever. Aggie was more relaxed. She had spent many years acquiring horses, and today was just another excursion for her.

"Good morning," said George Pyke when they climbed out of the Land Rover. He had spent some time on his appearance this morning. His bushy head of hair was carefully combed and plastered down, and he was wearing a shirt and tie beneath his jacket.

"Good morning," said Aggie, smiling warmly, her best foot forward to be as charming and persuasive as possible.

Susan was relieved to see that her mother, who liked to lie in on Sunday mornings, hadn't surfaced. The last thing she wanted was her mother offering to show them around the house, pointing out all the spiky hot-house flowers.

Diablo was led out of the stable. He didn't seem to sense that his future was the focal point of the activity. He was his usual arrogant and bad-tempered self, swishing his thick black tail, rolling his eyes to show the white rims, and laying his ears back threateningly to the world at large. He was saddled up quickly, and Porsche declared that she didn't want to see him ridden. She would try him herself. She swung herself into the saddle, and Diablo moved uneasily beneath her. Perhaps he sensed that he had met his match. Porsche was as bad-tempered and arrogant as himself.

They went out into the field, where there were a few jumps set up.

"Can you put them up to a decent height," commanded Porsche as if they were her servants there to do her bidding.

George hurried forward. He was obviously a little bewildered by the attitude of these grand visitors. He almost touched his forelock obsequiously. Susan felt helpless. She didn't like this at all. But at least she wasn't having Aggie and Porsche see her own humble little house on the development with boring old Barty.

Diablo cantered around the field with Porsche welded to the saddle. Susan had never seen anyone with such a strong seat, wondering if this young woman had ever fallen off. It seemed doubtful. Aggie kept up a stream of gentle, amusing patter, working her magic effortlessly.

"You should have seen your Susan on Sassy Swoop yesterday. Do you remember seeing her jump at Blossom Park last week? She was ridden by my Mercedes."

George grunted. He didn't want to admit that he couldn't remember the mare because he had been too busy drinking beer with his chums in the marquee.

"Would you be interested in a straight swap?" asked Aggie, "assuming that Porsche gets on with this fellow?"

"Hmmph," grunted George, not knowing what to say. He was entirely out of his depth in this situation. Perhaps he should be flattered by these august personages descending on him with such clear designs on Diablo. He wouldn't be too sad to see him go. Although Susan had acquitted herself admirably when she had ridden him at the point-to-point last year, and then at Blossom Park, he knew that it had been a case of touch and go. And the horse was undoubtedly too much for himself. Even if he were lunged for an hour before he rode, he never felt comfortable on him.

"Of course, if you think Diablo is worth more than the mare, then we could pay an additional sum," said Aggie, thinking perhaps that George wanted to make a sharp deal. Susan smiled to herself. Her father was no horse coper, and he was totally out of his depth.

"I think that Diablo is probably worth an equal amount," she chipped in. She had seen now that Aggie was the key to her social future. She liked

Porsche and certainly hankered after being her 'friend', but she doubted that Porsche ever gave one careless thought to having 'friends'. They were irrelevant to her.

Diablo and Porsche were now zooming around the field. They were probably going too fast, but Porsche drove the big horse on, forcing him to outrun his bad temper. They turned towards an upright post-and-rails set at four-feet six-inches, and relentlessly Porsche rode him at it as if they were in a race. He was galloping now, and they took off at least a good stride before it was necessary. The big black horse jumped as if he was determined to clear the moon.

"Goodness! He has got a jump in him!" exclaimed Aggie.

"Yes, he's some horse," said George, in a token effort to talk up the horse which he now seemed to be getting rid of.

"Would you like to come over and see Sassy today," said Aggie, smiling at him in her most winning manner.

"I don't think you need to see her, Daddy," said Susan. "I can vouch for her. She's not only gorgeous, but she's a fantastic fun ride."

George looked at Aggie and then his daughter and blinked like a rabbit caught in the headlights.

"I suppose I can take my Susan's word for it," he said.

"What do you think, Porsche?" called Aggie.

Porsche turned towards them.

"Yes, I want him," she replied.

"Well, then that's settled," said Aggie beaming at everyone.

Susan knew that she and her father had been railroaded, but she didn't care. She was to have Sassy Swoop, who really was the most darling of all horses. Throughout her childhood, there had been a long string of 'new horses'. Each one was meant to be 'the one' but had somehow turned out just as disappointing as the preceding one. Now, she knew that Sassy Swoop was to be the ultimate gorgeous horse. She was to be her consolation prize after bagging such a mistake of a husband.

"Daddy, I'll take the horsebox over with me. We can take Diablo, and I'll pick up Sassy Swoop," she said, now that it was all settled.

Poor George Pyke nodded his head. He had been cornered by three women. Game, set and match.

"What a good idea," said Aggie, who wanted everything settled. "I'll tell you what, we had a special saddle made to fit Sassy. She has a rather short back. That's the Arab blood in her. You can have the saddle as part of the deal," she continued with a magnanimous smile. "Then, I'll get Austin to drop your car back when he returns to Oxford with his chums."

Susan froze at this idea. What if Austin drove her car to her horrid little house on the outskirts of Rychester? It would be just too humiliating. What if Barty were there and she had to introduce him?

"No, Daddy can drive the horsebox, and I'll take my own car home," she said hastily.

It was all settled swiftly, and Susan thought that neither Aggie nor Porsche had thought of ever seeing her again. She had served her purpose. However, she was determined to stake a claim.

"I wondered, whether as part of the deal, I might be able to bring Sassy back to your place and school over your jumps," she asked.

"Of course, my dear, feel free to bring the mare over whenever you like," said Aggie, beaming at her.

Susan smiled. Now she could return to Pevensy Park whenever she wanted. She would become part of the large group of people who circled the Pevensy family like a school of fish in the swirling sea of plenty.

George Pyke drove the horsebox over, and when Aggie invited him to lunch, Susan declined on his behalf. She didn't want him blundering around, just in case he put his foot in it.

She did accept the lunch invitation herself. It was served outside in the garden. A delightful repast of salads and cold cuts. Not a traditional Sunday lunch at all. She was surprised when Austin sought her out.

"I say, Porsche is chuffed about that black horse. We sure appreciate it," he said, with a jovial hint at an American accent.

"I'm very happy with Sassy Swoop," said Susan primly. "I'm looking forward to coming over to practise jumping some of your cross-country fences."

"Jolly good," he said. "I guess we'll be up against you at the next hunter trials."

"When is the next event?" asked Susan casually.

"I think there's one over at Tiddington after Christmas. It's quite a distance, but we can go the day before and set up camp," said Austin, with a charming smile. Susan would have loved to have read something into this idea. "Of course, there's the point-to-point at Grassmere in three weeks. Do you think you might compete there?"

"I'll just come over and watch. Cheer you on," said Susan.

"Good-oh," he said with a smile, crinkling up the corners of his eyes, and drifted off to chat to his college friends.

This family is far too charming for the good of everyone else, thought Susan. Nevertheless, she was determined that she would wriggle her way in. Whether it be Aggie, Porsche or Austin, she would cultivate the friendship but make sure that Barty never got a look in.

Chapter Five – Half-Term at Pevensy Park

The youngest Pevensy child, Morgan, was twelve years old and suffered from being an afterthought. She stood outside the tight-knit family group as an observer. She approved of her two eldest siblings but didn't think much of Austin and Porsche. She judged that Royce and Mercedes were upright, decent, well-liked and respectable. In her opinion, Austin and Porsche were like terrible twins, egging each other on from one escapade to another. Austin was likeable and reckless and could charm the birds off the trees. Porsche's sole purpose in life was to be the best rider in the world, and she didn't care who she had to trample over to achieve this ambition.

Morgan, five years younger than Porsche, was treated as the baby of the family. This infuriated her. She didn't want to ride competitively. She had a passion for art, drawing beautifully detailed sketches of wildlife. Her other interest was motor cars, which she had got from her father. While Aggie was out being active in the community Morgan and her father tinkered with motors in one of the barns that had been converted into a garage-cum-workshop.

Aggie couldn't accept that Morgan didn't share the family's love of all things horsey, and she had manoeuvred Morgan into a friendship with Lavender Ellison-Heath. It was the ponies Black Boy and Rapide who had initially brought Morgan and Lavender together. Black Boy and Rapide had been the beloved and famous ponies of Jill Crewe. She had sold them to a family so that they could stay together, but it hadn't worked out, and they had been separated and lost each other.

The story about how they had miraculously been brought together again when they were both at Chesterton Show is narrated in the previous book *Jill's Ponies: Black Boy and Rapide*. Black Boy had carted Lavender out of the showjumping ring to find Rapide standing in the collecting ring. Morgan had found this vastly entertaining, and it had given her a good excuse not to do her showjumping round that day.

Aggie had sensed a unique opportunity and had taken Lavender's mother, Evelyn, under her wing. It hadn't taken a Freudian psychoanalyst to see that Evelyn Ellison-Heath was friendless and had no circle of intimates. She was the sort of woman that people avoided and made fun of behind her back. Aggie couldn't care less about Mrs E-H's unfortunate manner of exaggerated speech, tortured vowels and screeching. She understood that the poor woman was probably hiding some sort of unfortunate upbringing and wished to become part of the county set. Thus, the Duchess had set about drawing Mrs E-H into her circle of do-gooding ladies who sat on endless committees and basked in the glory of raising money for worthy causes. She was more than happy to exercise her power and promote Mrs E-H into a happier social position if it meant that Lavender might encourage Morgan into the world of equestrian competitions.

Morgan understood exactly what her mother was up to and had manipulated the situation so that Rapide could go and live at the Ellison-Heaths' place while she was away at boarding school. She had encouraged Lavender to enter Rapide in the Blossom Park Hunter Trials. It had all worked out beautifully with Ruby Swope being enlisted to work as a part-time groom, giving this young girl a fantastic opportunity to ride.

Ruby was often referred to as a gipsy, which was not technically correct. She lived in a dilapidated caravan with her mother in Ditching Hollow, an area never frequented by the middle classes. She had been the most faithful and industrious helper at Mrs Darcy's riding school, which was how Lavender had originally met her. She had come to Aggie's attention, through a friend whose daughter rode at the riding school, and in the spirit of doing good in the local community, Aggie had recommended that Ruby be employed as a part-time groom to help look after Black Boy and Rapide. In the normal course of events, Mrs E-H would not have countenanced the idea that Lavender had any association with such a girl as Ruby, but when 'dear Aggie' suggested it, she had complied without demur.

Now, the three young girls were to spend half-term at Pevensy Park with Black Boy and Rapide. This was the most tremendous experience for Ruby, who had found herself swept not only into Lavender's middle-class world but now the privileged domain of the local aristocrats.

Ruby, Lavender and Morgan were a merry trio, enjoying the 'otherness' of each other's company. They were all twelve years old. Morgan went to a posh boarding school, Lavender attended a private day school at Birtle, and Ruby went to the local school in Chatton. They were vastly different in terms of social background, but this didn't matter at all to the young people. Morgan was the daughter of a Duke and Duchess and lived in a huge house, like a stately home, the youngest child of a large family. Lavender was an only child and lived in a horribly modernised house that her mother thought was 'just the thing' in Chatton. Ruby lived in a sordid hamlet in a tumbledown caravan with a mother who was always poorly with a wracking cough and a father who occasionally turned up and made life even more uncomfortable.

The disparity in the girls' backgrounds and living circumstances seemed to enhance their small friendship circle, and there was no ganging up of two against one. Lavender was as shy and modest as Ruby was outspoken and curious. Morgan was always smiling wryly as if she were enjoying a private joke.

All three of them were to go to a Birtle Pony Club rally. Morgan had been a member since she was a tot but had managed to escape most of the activities over the years. It was to be Lavender and Ruby's first foray. They had read a lot about what went on in pony clubs, and on their first night at Pevensy Park, they badgered Morgan for more details. They were all sleeping in Morgan's room. She had gladly given up her enormous bed to Ruby, who observed that it was as big as her caravan. Lavender slept in the spare bed that was positioned beneath the window that looked over the park, and Morgan hunkered down on a trundle contraption that had been dug out of one of the numerous spare rooms full of odd pieces of furniture that had accumulated over the years.

They had one day to themselves before the rally on Saturday, and Morgan insisted that they climb the oak tree in the park where her tree house nestled in the branches. This was her private domain where she could escape from her family. Afterwards, she took them on a tour of the estate. Lavender was eyeing the cross-country course which she loved practising over, but Morgan insisted that the ponies have a day off before the rally.

The rest of the estate was utterly lavish. The tour included the nine-hole golf course, hard tennis court, and even a mini private aerodrome that hadn't been used in years. They ended up back in the garden. Ruby was looking at the view of the fields where the mares and young horses were grazing and found herself stepping into space and dropping into soft green velvet grass five feet below.

"Wot 'appened?" she called up to the others who were staring down at her in astonishment.

"You fell over the ha-ha!" said Morgan.

"There's no need to laff at me," said Ruby.

"No, the ha-ha is the name of the bank. It is designed to prevent an unsightly fence from spoiling the vista," explained Morgan, leaning down and offering her hand to pull Ruby back up onto the level of the garden.

"Let's go inside, there's a billiard room, and then there's a games room, kind of - a darts board and table tennis.

"You're as brave as they come," commented Lavender, "I'm sure if I fell that far I would be weeping."

"They breed us tough down at Ditchin' 'ollow," said Ruby.

"Before we go to hang out in the games room, I want to show you my totally favourite room. You can look, but you mustn't touch anything. Daddy likes it all just so," said Morgan.

Ruby and Lavender were astonished. The room was tucked discreetly beyond a bend in a long corridor. It was decorated as a Jaguar car, painted British racing green with two white GT stripes, with the brown leather upholstery and wood inlaid panelling. There was a painted wood-grain dashboard on one wall with a swinging speedometer that sped up from 0 and hovered around 100 mph. Morgan pressed a button, and they could hear a soundtrack of a roaring car, which they were told was the impressive noise of a Jaguar XJ12.

Morgan's father, the Duke, appeared in the doorway.

"This is 'mazin," said Ruby.

He smiled shyly.

"Why don't you take your friends driving, Morgan dear," he suggested.

"Oh yes!" said Morgan enthusiastically. "Come on, you lot. Daddy, can you come and get me started."

They trooped down to a large garage that was hidden behind a hedge on the other side of the house from the stables.

"Daddy lets me drive his little VW beetle," confided Morgan.

"It's such a divine colour, a sort of baby blue," remarked Lavender.

"Climb aboard," called Morgan, pushing back the left-hand passenger seat so one of them could clamber into the back seat.

"I'll go in the back," said Lavender, feeling that it might be safer, although on second thoughts if she wanted to jump out, it would have been easier to be in the front passenger seat.

Ruby settled herself in the front.

"Do up your seat belt," hissed Lavender in her ear.

"I do believe you're doubting my driving ability," said Morgan merrily.

The Duke had wandered off to polish up the bodywork on one of his shining Jaguars at the back of the shed.

"Hold tight, everybody. This thing always does start with a jerk," shouted Morgan, letting out the clutch and giving the accelerator a hefty push.

Lavender and Ruby bumped backwards as the car leapt uneasily forward. They were out of the garage and on the road that led around the park.

"I think I would rather have gone around the cross-country on a pony," said Lavender nervously.

"This is t'riffic!" said Ruby enthusiastically. "Do ya think you could teach us to drive?"

"We'd have to ask Daddy, but he was happy to give me lessons," said Morgan, who was concentrating on her steering. The little bug swerved sharply to the right as the track swung around, but they veered off the road, and Morgan had to correct their course.

"Look, there's that Porschey on the devil 'orse," said Ruby.

"No, Morgan, don't look, concentrate on driving," pleaded Lavender.

Diablo did look magnificent, clearing the high end of some of the cross-country jumps.

"She's riding in the point-to-point on Sunday," said Morgan, "probably giving him a last practice before the big event."

"She is very bold," said Lavender.

Finally, after veering from one side of the road to another on several occasions, they got back to the garage, and Morgan pulled up with a jerk in front of the double doors.

"Did you enjoy yourselves?" asked the Duke, coming out to see them.

"It was bang-on super," said Ruby enthusiastically. "I can't wait til I can learn to drive."

"Very interesting," said Lavender, who had jelly legs and felt as if she were going to collapse.

When Lavender recovered her strength from the roller-coaster ride around the park, she suddenly remembered.

"We have to clean our tack for the rally tomorrow. I believe that clean tack is probably the most important thing about going to a pony club rally."

Morgan groaned. "Now I remember another reason I hated pony club. The dreaded saddle soaping regime! I don't suppose we could rely on Tom and the others doing it for us."

"No, we cannot," said Lavender firmly. "It's a must-do ritual. I want to do it as other children do in the books."

They found the tack cleaning equipment carefully arranged in a large wooden box in the saddle room. Each of them armed themselves with a damp chamois, and they wiped down their saddles and bridles and removed any sweat marks and dirty grease. Then they pulled everything apart. The irons were removed from the stirrup leathers, which were taken off the saddle. Girths were unbuckled and put aside for special treatment, as a stiff, dirty leather girth was the cause of girth galls. The bridles were entirely dismantled, and they set to work wiping every piece of leather with the chamois before carefully applying saddle soap and rubbing it in with vigour, working their way around the buckles and keepers and making sure that no saddle soap was left on the metal parts or in the buckle holes. The stirrup irons and bits were washed and then dried and polished. They each took a clean, soft cloth and wiped down the leather, polishing it until it shone with a pleasing soft lustre. Then they reassembled the bridles and put the stirrup leathers and irons back on the saddle. Each checked the work of the others. All the strap ends were carefully tucked into the keepers.

"There's nothing more satisfying than cleaning one's tack to perfection," said Lavender.

"You think?" taunted Morgan.

They had supper that night in the nursery with Miss Penwith, the Pevensys' retired nanny, who listened with attention to Ruby and Lavender's excited chatter about their first pony club rally. She was knitting a jersey for Morgan. It was a jolly bright orange colour with turquoise stripes.

"I wish I could knit," said Ruby, who had been beset with a desire to learn every new skill that was being practised around her.

"Let me teach you," said Miss Penwith kindly. She had taken a shine to this bright little button of a child and was pleased that Morgan's friends were such interesting little creatures and not stuck-up and spoilt like some of the children's friends who had visited in the old days.

She found a pair of needles and a ball of left-over bright blue wool and cast on 40 stitches.

"In the beginning, you can just do knit, not purl, and you can make a scarf," she said. Carefully she showed the way to do the stitches, and Ruby watched attentively. She was soon struggling along, dropping a lot of stitches, and Miss Penwith would have to take over and retrieve them. However, the scarf was at least two inches long by the end of the night when the girls were shooed off to bed.

Lavender woke early the next morning. It was still dark outside, and the other two were sound asleep. Lying very still, she imagined the rally. She hoped that the other members would be friendly and that Black Boy and Rapide would enjoy themselves. It was almost as good as a gymkhana for them. Lots of other ponies zooming around here and there. Surely it would be more fun than just hanging out in the field.

Tom was driving the horsebox with the two ponies and the faithful old hunter Troubadour. The girls travelled in the cab with him. Aggie and Lavender's mother would follow in the car later. Lavender was mortified to find that her mother was insisting on attending the rally, determined to make the acquaintance of other pony club mothers and volunteer for a role in the club.

The girls got up when the alarm clock rang at seven-thirty. They tucked into a wholesome breakfast in the kitchen. Cook plied them with bowls of thick porridge and cream, followed by plates of bacon, black pudding and eggs. Ruby was astounded at this lavish spread and worked her way through everything that was set before her.

"You need to build yourself up," said Cook, eyeing Ruby's skinny frame.

"Poor Black Boy is going to buckle at the knees having to carry you with such a big breakfast inside," said Morgan with a grin. She was to ride Troubadour, the aged hunter that was usually used by her father on the rare occasions that he needed a mount.

All three girls were decked out in the Birtle Pony Club uniform, which was a green shirt and yellow tie with a dark-green V-necked pullover. After breakfast, they dashed over to the stable and helped to load the two ponies and Troubadour.

"You know Porsche is instructing today," said Tom, slyly. He was a terrific fan of Porsche and knew that there was bad feeling between her and Morgan's little friends.

"What!" exclaimed Morgan. "Porsche won't have anything to do with Pony Club since she thinks she's all grown up."

"She told me yesterday," said Tom, smugly.

"Well, if Porsche is my instructor, then I'm getting a headache," said Morgan grimly.

Lavender and Ruby looked at each other, thinking about the way that Ruby had played a cruel trick involving green dye the night before Blossom Park Hunter Trials. Although Porsche would have no proof that it had been Ruby, she must at the very least suspect. None of this boded well for a pleasant day. Lavender stared out the window at the fields. Grey clouds were gathering in the sky, which was tinged with a strange poisonous yellow colour. She wondered if it poured with rain, would the rally be called off. Perhaps that would be for the best.

Chapter Six – First Pony Club Rally

They arrived at the pony club grounds. It was a rather splendid field, large, flat and open with a grove of oak trees under which a set of wooden yards had been built. It had been donated by a venerable old horseman who had left it in his will before the war, and successive generations of pony club members and their parents had spent a lot of time working on it. Several local children in the village, whose fathers were not farmers, were able to keep their ponies in the field on the condition that they picked up all the horse manure every week. There was even a wooden hut in which were stored, tables and chairs, bending poles, jump flags and numbers and other assorted equipment that was used in the great and noble pursuit of good horsemanship.

Tom parked the Pevensy horsebox near the yards. It was by far the largest horse transport vehicle, and the three girls cringed a little as their arrival would not go unnoticed. Lavender was sure this was another ill omen, a portent of disaster. She tried to rouse herself out of this black mood, thinking that a pony club rally was hardly the event for impending disaster, but she couldn't shake the foreboding.

"Do you know anyone here?" muttered Lavender to Morgan.

"Quite a few of them look familiar, but I can't remember their names. Just kids who have been around the gymkhana scene for years" replied Morgan.

"There's that girl who rides the pale palomino at Mrs Darcy's. I think her name is Angela," said Ruby.

"Oh, yes. I remember her. That frizzy gold hair that sticks out around her hard hat is pretty distinctive," said Lavender.

"She's a bit of a washout," muttered Ruby, who had been at the pointy end of some of Angela's barbs.

"There's Dougie," said Lavender. Unaccountably she felt more cheerful, having recognised at least two of the other riders.

"I love 'is pony, tha' grey is bewt," said Ruby.

"Look, there's that girl that won the junior open, she had a Cornish name, I think," said Lavender. "She's a brilliant rider."

"Don't look now, but there's Porsche over there, just arrived with that woman, your mother's god-daughter, Susan King," said Morgan.

"Mummy is there with them," said Lavender. "How embarrassing!"

"Let's get tack'd up and start ridin' round," said Ruby, always eager to get into the saddle.

They busied themselves with the ponies and Troubadour.

"This horse is so big I'm going to be towering above everyone in my group, standing out like a sore thumb," complained Morgan. "How did I get tricked into this? I've managed to avoid pony club rallies for two years now!"

They saw a military-type man arrive in a sleek saloon.

"There's Major Holbrooke," said Lavender excitedly.

"There you go again, getting pony books muddled up with real life," said Morgan, smiling at her.

A young boy on a scruffy pony trotted past.

"Colonel Butterworth says assemble at nine-thirty," he called to them.

Morgan mock saluted. The three of them mounted and began to walk around to warm up the ponies.

"Morgan! Never thought I'd see you at a pony club rally!" called one of the girls.

"Hello, Thea," said Morgan smiling. "These are my friends Lavender and Ruby."

"I saw you riding at the hunter trials on Jill Crewe's pony, Rapide. That's him, isn't it? And that's Black Boy," said Thea.

"That be right," piped up Ruby. "Wot's yore pony call'd?"

"This is Summer Fancy," said Thea. "He's my new show pony. Mummy and Daddy are sure that he'll get me to Harringay."

"He surely is," said Ruby.

Fancy, as he was usually called, was indeed a very pretty bay pony with black legs. He had a perfect head with a broad forehead decorated with a tiny white star, small, neat ears and large soulful eyes. His mane was so carefully tended that it looked like it would spring into perfect little plaits of its own accord on the morning of the show. His tail was luxuriant and thick, falling like a waterfall between his neat square hocks. He looked a little rotund, but that was often the way with show ponies.

"What's he like to ride?" asked Lavender.

"Like a clockwork mouse, obeys every aid without a toss of his head," said

Thea. "I almost wish that he'd shy, or nap, or something, just to prove that he's got some sort of mind of his own."

"Can he jump?" asked Lavender.

"Not allowed. Mummy says it might ruin his legs. We wrap him in cotton wool so that he doesn't get scarred or anything. I'm lucky I'm allowed to come to a rally, but Mummy will be in the colonel's ear, telling him how special Fancy is."

"Don't you want to jump or go in games?" asked Morgan.

"Yes, I adore gymkhana games. I would love to get to the Prince Phillip Cup, not some boring old showing class at Harringay. My old pony, Dumpty, was brilliant at bending and musical chairs. I could see him listening to the music, and then he'd drag me into the centre to find the nearest chair," said Thea. "But Mummy's got her heart set on showing classes. So, it looks like I'll be helping put the jumps up for the rest of you this afternoon," she said dolefully.

"Look out!" called Ruby as one of the ponies ridden by a small child was leaping about frantically, trying to escape a mother wobbling on a bicycle who had accidentally run up behind it. The handlebars were tangled in the pony's thick matted tail. Porsche and Susan hurried over to sort it out. Susan grabbed the pony's bridle and attempted to control it while Porsche shouted at the hapless mother to get her bicycle away.

"Five minutes to roll call," said the colonel in a booming parade ground voice.

"Come on, let's get over there. Mummy and Daddy are watching from their car," said Thea, nodding her head towards a dark blue car parked down near the trees. "They watch me like a hawk all the time."

"My mother is here too," said Lavender, "she's over there."

"I saw your sister riding at the hunter trials. It's as if she's possessed by a demon, the way she jumps," said Thea to Morgan.

"That pretty well covers it," said Morgan. "Although I think she is a demon, not just possessed."

Twenty ponies and riders converged in the centre of the field.

"Good morning, boys and girls," the colonel boomed. "I want you to form a line."

There was a general shuffling around with a lot of flattened ears, rolling eyes, tails swishing, and children scolding and thumping their ponies with their heels, pulling their reins this way and that. Two mares were squealing at each other, and one was attempting to strike the other with her foreleg.

Their riders were bright red in the face but seemed powerless to do anything to stop this undesirable behaviour.

"Get those mares away from each other," roared the colonel.

Eventually, the ponies and riders were arranged in a ragged line.

"Now," said the colonel. "The teams' competition in the hunter trials. Some of you acquitted yourself creditably at Blossom Park, but if we're to make a good showing at regional finals at the beginning of December, there is a lot of work to do. I'm going to select the teams now, and those people will work with me, and the others will go with Miss Pevensy and Mrs King and do some schooling."

"Gosh," muttered Lavender. "We're new. How will he know whether to choose us or not?"

"The colonel has magical powers of perception, and undoubtedly Mummy has been in his ear. She'll have earmarked Black Boy and Rapide, but I don't think Troubadour will be much of a prospect. He's twice as tall as the two of you. That should mean I'm out. Anyway, I'll be back at school," said Morgan smugly.

"Quiet you girls, stop chattering," said the colonel shooting them a murderous look. "The good news is that Lettie Tregarth on Cornish Boy, who won the junior open at Blossom Park, is here today as a new member, along with Lavender Ellison-Heath and Ruby Swope. They're going to make up a new team, and we're expecting great things from them."

"Mummy strikes again," said Morgan with a derisive twist of her lips.

"How can them 'spect great thin's from me," muttered Ruby, her usual bright self-confidence suddenly dimmed by the huge expectation being heaped upon her.

"Those three make their way to the right," said the colonel.

Lavender went bright red with embarrassment as she rode forward out of the line, with Ruby and Black Boy beside her. She hoped that Lettie Tregarth wasn't aghast at having been clumped together with the novice newbies.

Lettie was older than both Lavender and Ruby. She had a mop of bright brown curly hair and looked very boyish. It crossed Lavender's mind that she could be George out of the Famous Five books. Cornish Boy was a tough-looking pony, not pretty but workmanlike. He was just under 14.2 hh, plain brown, with strong clean legs and a pleasant face with a bit of a Roman nose. Lettie smiled at her two new partners. Lavender and Ruby smiled back shyly.

"Next, we have the team that came second at Blossom Park," said the colonel. "Make your way over to the right."

Three children rode forward. These were Christopher and Catriona Hennington, brother and sister, riding their matched pair of chestnuts, who were both by the famous local pony stallion, Flying Dancer. With them was Merry Barton, who was riding another chestnut called Frolic.

"Gosh! They do look similar, don't they!" said Lavender.

"It would certainly help that two of them are from the same family and the ponies know each other so well," said Lettie with her Cornish accent.

"Where be you from?" asked Ruby curiously.

"We've just moved up from Helston, which is down south. My father is in the Navy," said Lettie.

"You know that Black Boy and Rapide have been stable mates forever. They used to belong to Jill Crewe, who was a well-known rider in these parts," said Lavender.

"Oh, my golly gosh! Of course, I've read the Jill books. Wait til I write to my friends in Cornwall that I'm in the same team as Black Boy and Rapide. They'll be well impressed!" exclaimed Lettie. "Do you hear that Corny, you're in the same team as two very famous ponies?"

The colonel then called out the team that had come fourth at Blossom Park, and the three teams were instructed to circle together.

"We can enter two teams in the regional finals, so we'll train you nine and make a decision closer to the date of the event," said the colonel. "We're going to do some exercises so that you can practise being together. I've got a long ribbon for each of the teams. You hold it in your hand. Do not wind it around your wrist! We'll see which team can end up with each member still holding onto the ribbon."

"I'm glad that we not tying it to our saddles," said Lavender.

Ruby and Lettie hooted at the thought of the chaos that might ensue should the saddles be tied together, and they separated.

"This gonna be fun!" said Ruby.

"First, I want you all trotting in a circle in your three teams. The trick is for the inside pony to be collected up and the outside pony to extend a little. Round you go! Use your noggins and try and get it right," commanded the colonel.

"Let's put Black Boy in the middle, and we'll ride on either side," said Lettie.

" 'e's tha meat in tha san'wich," tooted Ruby.

Black Boy seemed quite happy to be in the middle of the pack. He even seemed to match his stride to the others. Lettie collected up Cornish Boy, who had a long stride. Mrs E-H had come over to watch, and every time they rode past her, she waved at them. Lavender groaned. Lettie grinned at her.

The colonel called in each group of three and gave them a few individual pointers.

"You've got a push-button pony there," he said to Lavender, "and you have a correct position, but you're like a show rider, all arranged properly, but not making an effort to get the very best out of that pony. Imagine if you were riding a recently broken-in pony, or an untrained one, then sitting pretty is not going to do you much good. You need to sit down deeper in the saddle and try and feel what each leg is doing beneath you. You'll find it easier to give the aids at the exact moment if you know which leg is moving beneath you, especially in a transition from trot to canter."

To Ruby, he said, "you're trying very hard, and I can see that you're a natural. Well done, young lady. Just one tiny point, you tend to ride with straight arms as if you're pushing a pram. Remember to bend your elbows so there is a straight line from your elbow to your wrists to the bit. Keep up the good work." Ruby went bright red. She was at a loss for words.

"Lettie, it's the first time I've seen you ride, except for a flash as you galloped through the finish of the junior open. You and that pony have a very good relationship. You know, I think it might be good for all three of you to swap mounts. That way, you get to know each of the ponies in the team."

After a quick whispered discussion, they decided that Ruby should ride Rapide, Lavender on Cornish Boy and Lettie on Black Boy. They altered the stirrup lengths and mounted and continued to trot and canter around the larger circle while the colonel talked to the other riders. They noticed that none of the others was asked to swap mounts, but the Hennington brother and sister and Merry Barton each had to cross their stirrups and keep trotting and cantering without them.

The threesome that had come fourth at Blossom Park were Oswald Leadbetter, Jemima Grimsby, and Penelope Fletcher riding an ill-assorted collection of ponies, a grey, a brown and a skewbald. They were listening to some animated advice from the colonel with a collective mulish expression. Then, the colonel called everyone in.

"Now, to finish up this session, we'll have you going over a couple of jumps. There's a pile of forty-four-gallon drums over there. One member of each group should hold the ponies, and the other two run over and roll the drums to make a line, then back onto the ponies and circle twice and then over the jumps. You can each hold the ribbon and we'll see if you stick together."

Ruby held the reins, and Lavender and Lettie ran over with the Henningtons, Jemima and Penelope. They made two jumps, each consisting of four drums, then a barrel at each end to make a sort of wing.

"Now back up on the ponies, take a hold of the ribbons, canter a couple of times in a very wide circle, not over the jumps, and then on the third round, you can go over. Quick sticks!" instructed the colonel.

"May we take our stirrups back, sir?" asked Christopher.

"I suppose so," agreed the colonel.

Each team cantered around and over the drums. Lavender, Ruby and Lettie managed to stick together pretty well and keep hold of the ribbon. Lettie was pushing Black Boy on to keep up with the two bigger ponies, and Lavender had to adjust to Cornish Boy's long, rough stride. He was a good pony, but he had a straight shoulder which made his paces quite uncomfortable. She found she had to work a lot harder to ride him than the perfectly trained and amenable Black Boy and Rapide. The colonel had given her very wise advice!

"Lunchtime!" called the colonel after each threesome had jumped the barrels three times but first come over and listen to what I've got to say."

"I want you all to attend extra sessions which will be taken by the Hon. Miss Porsche Pevensy. Saturday afternoon at Pevensy Park every week until selection day. Is there anyone here who won't be able to attend?"

"I have tennis lessons every Saturday afternoon," whined Oswald.

"Speak to your parents. Get them to give me a ring," said the colonel crisply. "Now, here's a piece of paper and pen. I want each of you to write down your name, the name of your pony, your address and telephone numbers. Mrs Susan King will be assisting Miss Pevensy, and she'll contact each of you."

Ruby and Lavender looked at each other in dismay. If Porsche had anything to do with it, there was no way they were going to be selected to represent the club at the finals. She would humiliate them at every turn!

During lunchtime, Ruby and Lavender realised that it wasn't only Porsche who was against them. The other Pony Club members were distinctly unfriendly. The two teams who had competed at Blossom Park had assumed that they would be chosen for the regional finals and their collective noses were decidedly out of joint. The clank of ranks closing drifted through the air across the field. They hurried over to see Morgan, taking Lettie with them.

"How was your morning?" asked Morgan with a sardonic smile.

"We're practising for a shot at the regional finals. This is Lettie. Do you remember she won the junior open at Blossom Park? She's just moved here from Cornwall," said Lavender. "Lettie, this is Morgan Pevensy. She's actually the owner of Rapide, the pony that I ride, but she's on her family's faithful old retainer, Troubadour, today. The training sessions are to be held at her family's place."

"Good-oh!" said Morgan, giving Lettie a friendly smile. "This is Jo and Mary. We've all been in Porsche's group being given the treatment this morning."

"You'd think with her being your sister, she would have been a bit easier on you," said Jo, with a puzzled expression. "She really hit you with some criticism."

"That's our Porsche," said Morgan carelessly, for Porsche had attacked her mercilessly in front of the rest of the class.

"Porsche and Susan are going to be coaching the three possible teams for the regional finals," said Lavender with a grimace.

"Oh! Poor you! I told you that competing in horse events is not for the faint-hearted," said Morgan. "Thank goodness that I'm back at school!"

"I never thought I'd be in a team," said Ruby. "My first day at Pony Club."

"Don't forget you're riding the awesome Black Boy," said Lavender. "I'm sure he understands everything that the humans around him say."

"Well, the bad news for me is that I've got to sit my 'C' test," said Lavender.

"Me too," added Mary, who was a jolly-looking girl with bright red curls that framed her cute, freckled face.

"A test?" queried Ruby.

"Yes, there's four tests, starting with 'D' which is easy-peasy, and you just have to be off the leading rein, know how to mount and dismount, then there's 'C', and you don't usually do your 'B' until you are fourteen."

"I fort pony club would be fun, but it's all so serious," said Ruby.

"Wait til you get to camp, then it's drill all the time," volunteered Jo. "But we make sure we have fun at night, midnight feasts and playing tricks on each other."

"Sounds like boarding school in the books," said Lavender.

They ate their sandwiches and shared biscuits and chocolate bars around. Lavender was glad that she was sitting in a group. There were six of them, and she felt the strength in numbers as there were a lot of sharp spiteful looks being directed at them from the rest of the members.

"Have you seen her mother?" was one remark that floated across the air to them. Lavender, always conscious of her embarrassing mother, was sure that it was directed at her. Today, of all days, her mother had donned a pair of green diamante-decorated glasses. Lavender wanted to stick her head in a hole in the ground and never come up for air. Utter mortification!

"They're probably referring to Mummy," said Morgan airily. "She was in a hurry this morning and forgot her jacket and has been wearing an old cardigan that was in the back of the car for the dogs."

The afternoon was a lecture from Henry Thurston, who was talking about minor ailments and treatment that could be given by owners. Then everyone had a go at bandaging. Troubadour was chosen as the model for bandages, and he stood quietly while the pony clubbers took turns wrapping lengths of bandage around his sturdy legs. Ann had come along to watch the fun.

"I don't know why Jill and I never came to pony club," she said cheerily. "It looks such great fun. Birtle isn't quite hacking distance, but Mummy could have had us driven here in the horsebox."

"You could come along and do some instruction if you like," said the colonel gallantly. He was rather admiring of Ann, who, although not a conventional beauty like Porsche, was so merry and likeable.

"Henry and I could certainly volunteer for camp next summer," said Ann. "Wouldn't that be the most tremendous fun, Henry!"

"Yes, Ann. Whatever you say," he said, smiling adoringly at her.

"I can be Noel, and you can be Henry," said Ann.

"Who is Noel?" asked Henry, never having read the Pullein Thompson books.

"I'll be getting the needle all the time," said Ann, laughing her head off at her own silly joke.

"Now I think that we will have a fun sort of quiz," said the colonel. "If Miss Derry would like to mount Troubadour, she will demonstrate a riding position fault, and you must guess which one it is."

Porsche and Susan had left before lunch, so they were not there to twist up their faces facetiously, possibly thinking that with Ann riding, there would be more than one fault at a time to pick.

The first fault chosen by Catriona Hennington was that Ann's toes were pointing down like a ballerina. The second found by Lettie was that she was looking down at the ground and not between the horse's ears. The third was more difficult. After scrutinising Ann carefully, it was Oswald who declared that her feet were too far forward and not hanging in a line beneath her hips.

"That's enough for today. You're all dismissed," said the colonel.

Most of the club members were hacking home together and left in a bunch yelling cheerios to the others. Troubadour, Rapide and Black Boy were loaded into the Pevensy horsebox, and the three girls bundled into the back seat. They sang *Ten Green Bottles* all the way home in raucous voices and generally agreed that Lettie was a good sort, Cornish Boy impressive, Black Boy and Rapide were sure to get to the regional finals, and Morgan admitted that pony club wasn't as bad as she had thought.

Chapter Seven – Grassmere Point-to-Point

Lavender felt as if she were tumbling from one important horsey event to another, without a moment to catch her breath as the Grassmere point-to-point was the day after the pony club rally. She had been stricken with foreboding the day before, but nothing catastrophic had occurred, even though the other pony clubbers hadn't been exactly welcoming.

Her dark mood lightened. At least at the point-to-point she was a mere spectator and wasn't going to have to leap around a spectacularly dangerous course of jumps, jostled in the middle of a bunch of horses with thundering hoofs and outstretched necks.

Aggie had insisted that the three young girls go with the horsebox so that they could act as helpers for the three Pevensy competitors.

"I want you to be on hand to help Mercedes, Austin and Porsche with the horses. I've given Tom the day off as he accompanied you to the rally yesterday. Also, you can walk the course and then watch the riders, and it will be instructive for you."

"Which horses are competing?" asked Lavender with polite interest, not mentioning that she didn't think that point-to-points were in her future.

Austin will be riding Firefly in the open. Mercedes will ride one of Colonel Butterworth's hunters in the ladies' race, and of course Porsche on Diablo."

"What happened to Mangala? Why isn't she riding him?" asked Morgan in a knowing voice, like a teacher asking a question to which they know the answer.

"You know perfectly well what happened to Mangala," replied Aggie crisply. "He has a minor leg injury."

"Oh! That's right. He broke down a week after Porsche's heroic wins at Blossom Park Hunter Trials," said Morgan smugly. She was referring to Porsche's debut ride on the hapless Mangala when she had ridden so determinedly that they had won not only the novice event but also the open.

"I bagsie help Mercedes, and one of you can have the great pleasure of attending Porsche," said Morgan. Lavender and Ruby looked at each other. Out of politeness, they said nothing.

Mercedes drove the horsebox, and Aggie followed in the Land Rover with an enormous picnic hamper and some of the gear. In the horsebox, Porsche sat in the front next to Mercedes. Austin squashed in the back with the young girls, elbowing them into one corner so he could stretch out his long limbs. They arrived in plenty of time to find a prime parking position where it was possible to sit in the horsebox and watch a good portion of the course.

"If it rains, we can spectate from here," said Morgan.

"Not if you're acting as grooms," said Porsche nastily, "then you'll be down at the finish with the rugs and lead reins to assist us as we come in."

Lavender stared at the outlines of the trees that had lost nearly all their leaves in the brisk autumn winds. She knew that she would have to volunteer to look after Diablo, as Porsche so hated little Ruby that it would be dangerous to leave the young girl at her mercy. Perhaps that explained her feeling of dread.

They unloaded the horses, left their warm rugs on, and tied them up to the side of the truck out of the wind. Hay nets and buckets of water were given to them, and Aggie arrived with Royce in the Land Rover.

"I see that you're all set up," said Aggie. "Now, Royce will stay here with the horses, and the rest of us will walk the course."

They set off, an ill-assorted bunch. Porsche and Austin were arm in arm, Mercedes and Aggie deep in conversation and the three young girls trailing behind.

"I like this course. It's challenging but honest," said Aggie. The jumps were in fact, wide and inviting but the numerous ditches, both in front of and behind the jumps, were huge and black, looking very ominous to Lavender. The fences were at least four-feet high.

"I don't think I want to be a point-to-point rider," said Lavender. "I'll stick to pony club cross-country courses. Perhaps Mummy had the right idea when she was thinking of a show pony."

They trooped back to the horsebox, and Susan King was there, hanging around anxiously.

"I had so wanted to walk the course with you," she said, her voice a little whiny as if she had been deliberately left out. "You know I rode Diablo around here last year. I might have been able to give you some pointers."

For a minute, Porsche looked disdainful, as if Susan were hardly in a position to advise her, but she smiled a little. Susan was a useful ally, and there was no reason to shoot her down.

"Yoo-hoo!" called Ann Derry, hurrying over to them.

"I say today is sure to be fun. Henry is on Dauntless, James Bush on Lancaster Bomber and Austin I hear that Firefly is going great guns at the moment, which is good as Gary Horton on the Red Hornet is also in contention."

"Horton is a jumped-up showjumper, hardly decent competition," sneered Porsche.

"What did you just say about my fiancé?" demanded April Cholly-Sawcutt, who appeared out of nowhere, just in time to catch the spiteful comment.

Porsche stared at her, entirely unrepentant. "He might sit pretty on a trained showjumper, but he's hardly up to the hurly-burly of a point-to-point race."

"My Gary will be up there with the best of them," said April loftily.

"Come on, girls," said Aggie firmly. "The proof of the pudding will be in the eating!"

"Let's not quarrel," said Ann, who had introduced the topic in the first place, "sportsmanship is the name of the game."

Susan looked from one face to another. She desperately wanted to say something to show her support for Austin but could think of no interesting comment with the hot words flashing back and forth.

"Susan, you're not riding Sassy Swoop in the ladies' race?" asked Mercedes politely.

"No, I've not really formed a partnership with her yet. I would rather do some cross-country or hunter trials," said Susan, who in truth had begun to lose her nerve for daring feats of horsemanship. The last time she had competed on Diablo, he had been dangerously out of control, and it had only been good luck that they had got around. She loved Sassy but cantering around on the pretty mare making a pleasing picture for the onlookers was more than enough to satisfy her.

"Oh, look! There's Clarissa Dandleby, well, Clarissa Moreton now. She's got Cecilia with her," said Ann determined to change the subject.

"Who is Cecilia when she's at home?" asked Porsche, annoyed that Ann seemed to know more people than her.

"She's Jill Crewe's cousin," said Ann as if any relation of Jill Crewe was well known.

"I remember her from the Jill books," piped up Lavender, "very keen on needlework."

"Yes, I always thought her friendship with Clarissa, who is so very horsey and unfeminine, was a strange combination," said Ann.

"Clarissa always seems to be mounted on a plain brown thoroughbred gelding," commented Mercedes. "It's a wonder she can tell which is which!"

"Well, by all accounts, she has the pick of her husband's jumping stable. It certainly suits her to be married to a trainer," said Ann.

Clarissa and Cecilia walked over. Clarissa strode in a mannish way. Her greasy hair pulled back in an unattractive bun. Cecilia was like a porcelain doll, picking her way carefully across the grass, making sure she didn't step in a pile of manure.

"Have you heard from Jill lately?" Cecilia asked Ann.

"Yes, she's slaving away at Porlock to get qualified as a riding instructor mixing with a bunch of other students from all around the world. Quite an international group!"

"I thought she'd been working as an instructor at Mrs Darcy's since she was about thirteen," said Cecilia.

"I know, but it's all the rage now to get qualified," explained Ann.

"I think that you've either got the skill or you haven't. Only those with no natural talent need to get trained," said Cecilia, who had never delivered a riding lesson in her life.

"I better get over to Colonel Butterworth's horsebox and get acquainted with my ride today," said Mercedes. "I've never even ridden the horse, just going to have to hop on and have a go."

"Oh! Look, there's Jackie Heath over there," said Ann, tripping across the grass to see her friend.

"Yoo-hoo, Jackie!" she called cheerily. "Are you riding in the ladies' race today?"

"Nope," said Jackie firmly, shutting down the suggestion.

Ann looked at her. Instinctively, she didn't ask about Jackie's twin sister, Val who was working for a wealthy horsey family in America.

"Is Henry riding?" asked Jackie, determined to change the subject away from herself.

"Yes, he's on his chestnut, Dauntless. I've been training him. I've walked literally miles around the lanes for weeks now. He had ligament trouble, and I was determined to strengthen his legs slowly and carefully."

"Why don't you ride yourself in these races?" asked Jackie.

"I don't know. I just feel happier being the helper or assistant," said Ann. "I like riding, communing with the horse and the countryside, but my competitive spirit, such as it was, has faded away. Not like Jill. She's going great guns. Always on a mission to improve herself and get out there and compete. How is Serena doing with the Miss Farthingtons' horse, Patchwork? It was such a good opportunity for her to get a horse to compete on, not just instructing at Mrs Darcy's."

"I think the plan was for her to give him some intensive dressage training, so I doubt she'll be roaring around in a pack jumping wildly," said Jackie. "I know that the old dears didn't want him to go to the riding school, so he still lives like a lord in the dining room and Serena cycles over every day to muck out and ride."

"Let's go and walk the course," said Ann. "I can see Henry looking around for me."

"No, I can't be bothered," said Jackie, "I'm going back to the car. It's too cold out here."

Ann hurried over to Henry, who was looking impatient.

"Oh, poor Jackie, she's such a gloom-bag," said Ann. "You know, I think she suffers from an inferiority complex. It's like her twin got all the get-up-and-go, leaving her deficient."

"You always want to help everyone," said Henry admiringly. "Right now, I need some of your expert advice on jumping this course."

Ann smiled at him fondly and put her arm through his. They set off to walk the course.

When all the course-walking was over, the spectators gathered at the rope that was strung along the finishing strip so that they could see the winners flash across the line. There was also a good view of the first four jumps before the riders swung around in a huge circle far out into the field. There were two races before the ladies' race, one for the locals who lived within a fifteen-mile radius and another for novice riders who had never ridden in a point-to-point before.

The competitors in the ladies' race and the open gathered in a bunch to watch how the course jumped. They screwed up their eyes and had technical discussions on how they were planning to ride.

Then, it was time for the ladies' event, and the horses and riders circled in front of the spectators. Mercedes was sitting atop a very tall horse, at least 17 hh, looking workmanlike and capable, seated in a perfect position. The horse she was riding was dark bay who walked with a long, clean stride, his powerful muscles playing and rippling under his glossy skin, with very large quarters, thick, strong hocks, and his impressive height he looked like a giant horse out of mythology.

"Gosh!" exclaimed Ann, "he's certainly an animal to be reckoned with. I thought with Porsche on Diablo; she was a certainty, but now I'm not so sure."

Diablo was as evil-looking as ever, rolling his eyes, flashing the whites at other horses, tossing his head, and swishing his tail. Porsche sat in the saddle confidently. It seemed as if nothing ever worried her. She was a young woman with no nerves when it came to riding. Her nature consisted of sheer determination.

Clarissa was mounted on the inevitable brown thoroughbred, but she didn't look half-bad. Her horse was undoubtedly fit and well-trained. Her boiled gooseberry eyes were gleaming as she walked him around the collecting ring, sizing up the competition. She didn't look fazed to be competing against the formidable Pevensy women. The other female riders included a tall, angular woman on a skinny grey mare who looked ready to be retired, along with her rider.

"She's always been a hard woman to hounds," said April to Ann in a perfectly audible stage whisper.

"Quite an age to be competing in this sort of competition," replied Ann.

"Born in the saddle and hunted three times a week all her life," replied April. "She knew Daddy well and used to come over and look out any of his horses that weren't considered suitable for showjumping."

"How is your father?" asked Ann, hoping this wasn't an awkward question. Captain Cholly-Sawcutt had been a cult figure for her and Jill when they were youngsters. He had competed in the British showjumping team many times and had got Jill to teach his three daughters to ride because they showed absolutely no aptitude, and he couldn't bear to watch their efforts. They were named April, May and June, and as young girls, they had been as fat and round as bouncing balls. May and June were still very much on the hefty side, but April had slimmed down amazingly and was now engaged to the dashing Gary Horton who ran the Cholly-Sawcutt showjumping yard because the Captain had dementia and was in a home, not remembering his illustrious career and some days not even recognising his family members.

"He only remembers Mummy these days," said April sadly. "He's on the downhill slope, I'm afraid."

"Oh April," said Ann, "I'm sorry, he was such a wonderful man. It is so odd having been one of the best showjumping riders in England, and now he can't even remember it."

"Look they're getting ready to start," said April turning her head away, changing the subject. The ten horses and riders were milling around along the length of the tape. They formed a line that moved restlessly back and forth, like an errant wave. The starter picked his moment, lifted his arm, and released the tape as he swung it down. They were off with an impressive thunder of hoofs.

Diablo and Porsche careered straight to the front and, veering dangerously, cut across the path of Clarissa and the old woman on the grey. Porsche obviously wanted a position on the inside rail so that they had the advantage when the course curved to the left. Mercedes kept her big horse to the outside, correctly anticipating Porsche's riding tactics.

"You thruster!" shouted Clarissa in an exasperated tone, forced to slow her horse down to avoid a collision.

"Get out of the way, gel!" shouted the old woman.

Porsche was bent over Diablo's neck making no attempt to check his wild gallop as he surged ahead of the other horses.

"She might be going too fast too early," said Morgan. "He'll run out of steam and have nothing left in the tank for the finish."

"You might be right there," said Ann. "That fat chestnut mare at the back is so slow she couldn't catch a cold!"

"She'll be first in the next race," quipped Aggie.

Clarissa was galloping steadily along in second position next to the old woman on the grey, whose horse's nose was level with Clarissa's brown gelding's shoulder. Mercedes was fourth but galloping wide of the rail, out of the way of Porsche and her desperate tactics. The other horses and riders were several lengths behind, with the fat chestnut trailing at the end of the field.

"That Diablo looks positively demonic," commented Ann. Everyone looked at the black gelding who had white foam frothing from his mouth, like a rabid dog. He was surging along ahead of the others snorting through flared nostrils like dark pits. He leapt each fence, landing with snapping legs that moved in short, brittle movements until Porsche pushed him on to lengthen his stride. He continued to pull and jerk at the reins, every muscle set with spiteful rage.

"Do you think he had a bad experience in his childhood?" commented Jackie, who had been reading books about Freud's psychodynamic theories.

Then the horses swung to the left and could be seen in the distance on the far side of the course. Aggie had a set of binoculars and gave a running commentary.

"Diablo is still in the lead, but the brown and the grey are not far behind. Now, Mercedes is moving up on the outside."

"I suppose she is giving Porsche a wide berth. She's just as likely to lash her sister with a whip if she attempts to pass her," said Morgan.

"Don't malign the family, cupcake," said Aggie.

"Cupcake!" snorted Ruby.

"I can't help the family I was born into!" retorted Morgan.

"Mercedes is drawing level, and the grey and the brown are only half a length behind. Diablo looks to be struggling," said Aggie, with a faintly discernible tone of satisfaction. Mercedes had always been her favourite child.

Susan King grimaced. She had wanted Diablo to win. If he let Porsche down she feared that their friendship might be over, as it was built on the shaky foundations of Porsche's desperate desire to be the best.

"They're coming around the bend to the home straight, just three more fences to the finish!" exclaimed April.

"They're all in a bunch. It's hard to see which is in the lead from this angle," commented Cecilia breathlessly. It was her first point-to-point, and she hadn't realised just how exciting was horse jump racing. "Oh! Do come on, Clarissa!"

They were leaping in a tight bunch over the last three fences.

"If one falls, they'll all go down," said Lavender, deciding that she was never going in a point-to-point race in all her life.

Over the last jump, Diablo rose in the air but he was tiring, and his legs dragged through the top of the brush. Porsche was flailing him with her whip, but he had no energy left. He had used up too much with his unreasoning anger and flashing spite. He veered to the right and stumbled as he landed. Clarissa's brown horse got bumped, and he, in turn, nudged the grey with the old lady. Mercedes had stuck to the outside all the way around to keep clear of trouble, and now she forged ahead. Down the home straight, she rode, straight as an arrow, still in a perfect riding position, with no need to ply her whip. Colonel Butterworth's tall horse was indubitably the winner. Mercedes had run a copybook race. Her cheeks were blooming with exertion, but she remained composed and smiled and waved at the cheering crowd.

Morgan dashed down with the lead rein to clip onto Mercedes' mount, and Lavender followed slowly, dreading her role as the helper for Porsche, who was sure to be in a filthy mood. Colonel Butterworth was thrilled with his horse's win, and he was huffing and puffing all over the place. Clarissa was second, and the old woman third. Porsche wasn't even in the line-up to receive an award which was probably just as well as she was not the sort to lose with good grace.

The final race of the day was the open. Henry, Austin, James and Gary had missed the excitement of the ladies' race as they had been preparing their horses, walking around to warm them up. Between them, there had been a lot of good-hearted banter, with each claiming that they were certain to win and handshake bets between them added extra excitement to the competition.

Ann was beside herself with excitement. Henry was so modest and unassuming. He had come second in the open event at Blossom Park hunter trials, and Ann believed in him.

Gary Horton looked arrogant and sniffy on The Red Hornet, a horse which was rumoured to have cost an enormous sum. Unusually, Gary had contributed half of the purchase price from his own funds. In the normal course of events, he let April pay for everything, but now he felt like he needed a personal stake, in case he found that when it came to it, he just couldn't bear to tie himself to April for life. He was getting sick of her proprietorial attitude. He had noticed Mercedes, not only her wealth and aristocratic pedigree but her wonderful cool riding style. April never got on a horse. She knew that it didn't show her off to best advantage.

James Bush had high hopes of his horse, Lancaster Bomber, which his sister, Diana had ridden at Blossom Park and surprisingly come fourth in the novice event. If truth be told, Diana was probably a more careful and competent rider than James, but he was the one brimming with ambition and bravado, and today he was determined to prove himself.

Austin was the wild card. He feigned carelessness and a casual disregard for winning, maintaining that he was only interested in the sport and excitement, but his mount, Firefly was a very classy horse, and it was possible that Austin would pull a rabbit out of his hat. In races like this there was a huge element of chance as the pack of horses thundered around the jumps. One horse falling could have a domino effect, and who knows who would win.

The competitors were milling around, and the starter watched the line ebbing and flowing against the tape. For one moment, they were lined up more or less in a straight line, and he dropped his hand, and the tape zinged back. They were off, and the crowd roared. Austin and Firefly leapt to the front and were into their stride within two lengths. Gary on The Red Hornet had carefully positioned himself on the rail, and he was on the tail of Austin with a deadly determined expression on his face.

The rest of the field bunched up behind them, James, Henry, and four other horses and riders. They maintained their position over the first four jumps and swept around the curve to the far side of the course. Ann had found a set of binoculars in the back of Henry's Land Rover and she kept up a running commentary as the race progressed.

"Austin is still in the lead, but Gary is gaining on him. Henry has drawn ahead of the bunch and one of the brown horses has fallen back and is trailing behind."

"It would be a turn-up for the books if Austin were to win," said Jackie. "I don't think he has ever actually won a race."

"Well, I don't suppose you've ever even entered one," snapped Porsche, who would always defend her brother.

"Come on, Gary, it must be time to make your move," said April, standing on tip-toe, trying to see what was happening.

"I think you're right. Gary is getting ahead. He and Austin are now side by side."

"Come on, Gary! Come on, Gary!" shouted April.

"Henry is gaining on them. Yes, yes, yes. I think he's going to do it," shouted Ann, leaping around.

Henry had risen to the occasion, and he was riding magnificently. He wanted to win for Ann, to show her that he was the man she would want to marry. Gary was spurred on by his arrogance. Secretly, he wanted to impress Mercedes. Austin was just racing for the hell of it. He was so sure of himself that he didn't feel that he had anything to prove to anyone. James was finding that he was out of his league. He was desperate to prove that he was more than a small-town rider who had risen to the top of a very small pond.

Ann was beside herself with excitement when Henry on Dauntless dashed past the finishing line first. She ran, harum-scarum, onto the course to lead him back down.

"You've proved yourself now!" she cried. "You can win on more than one horse!" She was referring to his previous win on Black Comedy.

Gary had come a close second on The Red Hornet. He had wanted so desperately to win, but at least this might get him noticed by the cool Mercedes. April had clipped the leading rein to his horse's bit and was bowing and waving to the cheering crowd as if it had been herself who had ridden the horse. Austin was third and rode back with a wide grin being led by Ruby who was enjoying this moment of reflected glory. Poor James hadn't even managed fourth. He had been at the tail end of the field, and a tall grey horse ridden by a tough-looking youth with sticking-out ears had come fourth.

Aggie had everyone go back to the Pevensy horsebox after the presentation and set out two picnic tables with delicious treats. Austin popped the corks of the champagne bottles and filled glasses. Everyone toasted first Mercedes and then Henry. April was busy chattering away but she didn't fail to notice Gary's eyes following Mercedes' slim figure as she moved around offering platters of finger food that had been prepared by the Pevensys' Cook.

Henry almost got carried away with the adrenalin of the race, the champagne but most of all the shining adoration in Ann's eyes and considered getting down on one knee and proposing. Then he remembered Ann's plan to go to Bristol to study to become a vet and decided that this would complicate her life, and he didn't want to put pressure on her.

When all the champagne was drunk and the nibbles demolished, the horses were tended to and put back into their transport, and everyone set off for home.

Chapter Eight – The Funny Old Farthingtons

On the day after the point-to-point, Lavender and Morgan had been hoping that they would have a chance to jump around the cross-country course in the park, but Aggie had other plans. She had instructed Cook to fill a basket with vegetables from the garden and then added a fat chicken, and several jars of honey from the beehives at the bottom of the orchard.

"I want you three to take this over and visit the Farthingtons and offer to help them with the animals. The poor old dears, they're so busy looking after their creatures, I'm sure they forget to feed themselves," said Aggie, in her brisk do-gooding voice. She went on to explain, "you know my mother-in-law, the previous Duchess was well-acquainted with their mother. She was a formidable woman. She lived until she was one hundred and three years old and used her daughters as companions. If she rang the bell, they had to go running upstairs to do things like pick up a handkerchief that she had dropped. Or she would ring the bell at two in the morning because she wanted hot milk. I imagine they would still flinch when a bell jingled and jangled. The poor dears never went out into society and had no chance to marry. Now they've taken refuge in their vast menagerie."

"But how could they endure it? You would think they would run away," said Morgan. "Did they have a father?"

"He died in the First World War," said Aggie. "The girls were devoted to their mother, completely subjugated to her strong will. In those days, they owned a dozen of the village cottages and lived off the rents. Now the cottages are sold, renovated out of all recognition, or knocked down. The money has all gone, and poor Felicia and Jessica spend the little that they have got on those animals which they have collected. I suspect that it is a substitute for the children they never bore."

They stopped outside a set of rusty, battered gates. You could see the old house dreaming in the distance. It looked like a fairy tale kingdom, old and half-asleep, enclosed by a high wall covered with moss and lichen. The tall cypresses rose like garden turrets, or perhaps like birthday candles, standing sentinel.

They rattled up the driveway. The gravel was sparse, and weeds poked their cheeky heads up along the edges of what had once been a smooth velvet green lawn. Now it was grazed bare by an ancient donkey that sheltered in the stunted shrubbery. Two pillars flanked the porch of the old house, their plaster was flaked and decayed and the four steps that led to the front door were grimy with dirt and moss. The terrace that ran down the side of the house was a mass of broken flags that threatened to trip and break the ankle of any unwary walker. Half a dozen dogs rushed out of the open front door, yapping and leaping about. They were mongrels of the first order, and it was difficult to discern exactly which breed or mixture of breeds they might represent. But not having distinguished pedigrees didn't seem to thwart their enthusiasm. Visitors were obviously an entertaining diversion!

"Such cute dogs!" exclaimed Ruby, patting them as they leapt up on her.

There was a rusty iron boot scraper beside the door, and Aggie instructed the girls to make sure their shoes were clean. An old lady appeared in the doorway. Elegant and tiny. She was as upright as a small knitting needle with a twist of soft, silver-grey hair on top of her head. She smiled, and her face lit up like a shining star. Greeting them in a soft musical voice, she led them down the passageway to what must have once been an elegant drawing room, dotted with faded and broken furniture. A few sagging curtains hung from the curtain rails. Others had long fallen off, rotted away on their hooks and probably put to good use as bedding for the various animals. Lavender's gaze ran wildly around the room, like a startled hare, from the dusty ornaments that were lined up higgledy-piggledy in an old-fashioned glass-fronted cabinet to the collection of small tables, some of which were lying on their sides. She feared that she might get optical indigestion. There was so much to see.

"Where's that 'orse?" asked Ruby.

"He's in the next room," said Felicia, smiling at her. "What a trio of little angels you are!"

Morgan snorted like an obnoxious pony. She thought that if Miss Farthington knew what they had all got up to she wouldn't think them angels.

"Give Miss Farthington the provisions dears," said Aggie. "We've brought you some supplies to keep you going in your wonderful work looking after animals."

"Oh, that is so thoughtful of you!" said Felicia, clasping her hands together.

"Tom is going to bring you over a trailer load of hay," said Aggie, "to feed that wonderful horse."

"Oh yes! Patchwork is progressing marvellously," said the old lady. "That lovely Serena from Mrs Darcy's comes over every day and trains him religiously. She's been working on his dressage, and we're thinking he might enter his first one-day event in the spring."

"I thought I'd leave the girls here for the day, and you could put them to work. They're very keen and love doing things with animals," said Aggie as if it had been the girls who had come up with this idea rather than herself.

"Oh, how kind!" said Felicia. "I'll just call for Jessica. I think she is out in the garden digging it over after our summer harvest. She would certainly appreciate a little youthful energy to help her."

The girls thought that digging in a garden didn't sound like the best fun in the world, but they were happy to help out if they could.

Jessica Farthington was as round and comfortable, as her sister was slim and elegant. She rolled into the room, her eyes shining with the same friendly welcome.

"Oh! We do love to see you, Aggie, not just for the goodies that you bring us," she boomed in a deep, jovial voice.

"Roast chicken for dinner. What a treat! The dogs will love the leftovers."

"The chicken is for you, not the animals," said Aggie laughing at them.

"Of course, of course," said Felicia soothingly. "Jessica was only joking."

"Would you like us to do some digging?" asked Lavender politely.

"Not digging," said Jessica. "But if you could muck out Patchwork's room, that would be very helpful."

"That soun's more like us," said Ruby, grinning at the old ladies. She thought they were brilliant, not like the other stuck-up grownups in the world.

"Lead the way," said Morgan, who was curious about this domestic arrangement for the horse. "Mummy we might consider moving our horses into the house."

"Oh Morgan! You're always the joker!" said Aggie mildly. "But I must admit that I'm curious to see how this arrangement works."

The Farthingtons led the way. It wasn't just a simple walk down the passageway. The house had been adapted for the needs of the care of animals. The hall was cluttered with sacks of corn, oats, barley and some bales of hay.

"Surely you have a feed shed for these supplies?" asked Aggie, unable to quell her managing instincts.

"I'm afraid the outhouses and stables are in such a state of disrepair that they're not suitable for use," said Jessica.

Aggie began to consider sending over a team of men to repair some of the outbuildings. She couldn't help herself. She loved to fix things.

Beyond the feed sacks were a series of makeshift pens in which a variety of puppies lived. The air was thick with a doggy smell.

"Where do all these puppies come from?" asked Ruby.

"People bring them to us," said Felicia.

Therein lies the problem, thought Aggie. The Farthingtons were known in the district for taking in any animals so people naturally brought them creatures of all kinds. They had become a useful solution to any unwanted animal problems.

They squeezed themselves past the pens and finally came to the dining room. Felicia opened the door and made a flourishing gesture with her hand.

"Here is our beautiful boy!"

He was indeed beautiful—an interestingly patterned skewbald with a bold curious head.

"He's totally fab!" exclaimed Lavender.

"The way he has white patches around each eye, with the rest of his face brown makes him look like he's wearing spectacles," said Morgan. "We saw him when Serena rode him at Blossom Park Hunter Trials."

"Yes, she is an absolute dear," said Felicia.

"Such a nice young woman," agreed Jessica.

The smell of horse was strong in the dining room, and Aggie could understand why they kept the door shut. Although it was questionable whether the doggy smell wasn't worse than the horse smell. The house was never going to be liveable again, and when the Farthingtons passed away, it would have to be demolished.

"Serena's doing some intensive dressage training on him now. She comes every day, you know to work him. Sometimes she just takes him out for a hack. She is very sensitive to his needs," said Felicia.

Aggie said she had to go, and the three girls found the mucking-out tools outside on the terrace. Patchwork entered and exited through the French doors. They set to mucking out with gusto. The dining room was much larger than the average loose box, so it took a long time to work their way around. Patchwork followed them, nudging them and nibbling at their pockets looking for titbits.

"Do you get the feeling that this horse is regularly fed sugar and apples?" asked Morgan.

"He's nearly ripped my jodhs," said Lavender. "I'm not sure it's such a good idea to treat a horse like a pet."

"He's gotta learn sum manners," remarked Ruby wisely.

Serena turned up as they had finished, and they watched as she saddled up the gelding.

"Wots 'e like to ride?" asked Ruby.

"He's challenging, but he's smart, and he learns so quickly," said Serena. "We've graduated to some lateral work. He got shoulder-in so quickly that we're now doing half-passes, but only at the trot."

Serena led Patchwork out through the glass doors, and he picked his way across the broken flags. There was a flat field beyond the garden. The gate was propped against the hedge. The hinges were long broken off. Serena mounted and rode around on a loose rein. Patchwork skittered a little here and there as small birds flew out of the ragged hedge.

"He's only messing around a bit. He's spirited," explained Serena.

"Spoilt rotten," commented Morgan.

After ten minutes, Serena shortened her reins and Patchwork sprang into a strong trot, covering the ground in great sweeping strides.

"He certainly doesn't move like he's pulling a grocer's cart," said Morgan.

"Is that what he used to do?" asked Lavender.

"That's what Porsche said, but she could have just been being catty," replied Morgan.

Serena worked Patchwork for forty minutes. She pushed him through bursts of hard work and then walked him on a long rein for several minutes. She rode back to the girls.

"Where did 'e come from?" asked Ruby.

"Apparently, one of the Miss Farthingtons' friends found him pulling a cart through the East End of London, and she purchased him from the man in the cart and put him on a train to Oxford. It took ages to get him healthy, and now he's been here for twelve months," explained Serena.

"Do you think he's got a chance of being a good eventer?" asked Morgan skeptically.

"Why not?" asked Serena. "Not all eventers have blue blood you know."

They helped her untack and rubbed him down. He was rugged with a tattered canvas rug and put in the small orchard where he could wander around during the day.

"He needs a horse companion," said Lavender, remembering how lonely Black Boy had been before Rapide had come to live with them.

"I don't think the Farthingtons should take on any more animals," said Serena lightly. "They put old Hector in with him sometimes. You know that donkey that you might have seen grazing in the front garden."

"I s'pose a donkey is better than nuffin," said Ruby.

Felicia came out of the house.

"How did Patchwork go today, dear?" she asked Serena.

"He's marvellous, so quick to learn, and he's settling down better. I thought we might have just one jumping session a week in the future," said Serena. "Now that his basic training has come on so well."

"Whatever you think," said Felicia.

"Now, you three little angels, I wondered whether you might like to teach the puppies to lead. We're going to put up a sign in the Chatton shop looking for good homes and thought that if they could be trained to lead a little, it might be easier to find them new owners."

"Sure fing," said Ruby. "Trainin' dogs can't be as 'ard as trainin' 'orses."

"Don't you believe it," said Morgan stoutly.

The puppies were full of life and leapt about exuberantly. It took ages to persuade them to accept being on the lead and endless patience to try and get them to walk obediently and stop trying to run away in short bursts.

"They're so gorgeous. I'm going to ask Mummy if we could have this one," said Lavender, who had fallen in love with a black, brown and white female who looked as if she were part sheepdog. "Look at her soulful eyes. I'm sure she's pleading to come home with me."

"Your mother doesn't seem like a doggy person," observed Morgan.

"Yes, but your family has a whole gaggle of dogs. I'm sure if I mention that first, she might be persuaded," said Lavender with a grin.

They sat down to eat their sandwiches and shared their crusts with the puppies who were crawling all over them, like ants on a honeypot.

Jessica came out and brought them two hard-boiled eggs each.

"Our hens have been laying very well lately," she said. "And these eggs are delicious. Look how yellow the yolks are."

"Scrumptious," said Lavender politely. "What would you like us to do next?"

"It would be wonderful if you could clean out the rabbit hutches, they're round the back near the vegetable garden."

"Sure fing," said Ruby, leaping to her feet.

The rabbits were big and fat. They came in all sorts of colours: grey and white, black, white and some beautiful dark grey, almost blue ones.

"What do you do with them?" asked Morgan.

"We eat them and feed them to the dogs," said Felicia.

"You eat them!" cried Lavender, looking at the pretty fluffy creatures.

"I know, dear. It is hard sometimes to wring their necks, but it's nature, and we do have to eat and feed the dogs," explained Felicia gently.

"Of course. It's only practical," said Morgan. "Mummy told me that during the war, they bred rabbits for meat, and Cook used to make the most delicious stews which they shared with people in the village."

After they had finished cleaning the hutches, which was difficult as they were not designed in a sensible manner, just a collection of boxes that had been adapted, Aggie arrived to pick them up.

"How did your day go?" she asked as she drove them back to Pevensy Park.

They gabbled on telling her about Patchwork, the puppies and the rabbits.

"What about tomorrow?" asked Aggie. "It's your last day."

Lavender and Ruby looked at each other meaningfully.

"I suppose we could ride," said Morgan reluctantly.

"Yes!" shouted Ruby.

"Whizzo!" said Lavender.

"There you go," said Aggie smiling to herself. It was part of her plan that the pony-mad Lavender and Ruby should encourage Morgan to get on a horse.

Chapter Nine – Training Day Disaster

Lavender and Ruby were not looking forward to the first coaching session for the regional finals. Porsche was not just a dark blot in their lives, she was an evil enemy. She seemed to especially hate Ruby. Considering it was Ruby who had coloured Mangala bright green the night before the Blossom Park Hunter Trials, this was hardly surprising. Porsche couldn't know for sure that it had been Ruby, but she was deeply suspicious. Lavender's feeling of dread from the first pony club rally had returned with a vengeance.

"She'll prob'ly design an impossible jump and make me jump over it, and it'll kill me an' Black Boy," moaned Ruby.

Lavender said nothing. She couldn't refute Ruby's suggestion as there seemed to be no limits to Porsche's spite and desire for revenge. They spent at least an hour grooming the ponies and then as much time cleaning their tack. If nothing else, there could be no criticisms of their appearance.

Lavender's mother was taking them in the horsebox to the coaching session. She had arranged to have afternoon tea with Aggie.

"It is a great honour to be picked for this training," she said as she wheeled the horsebox through the gates of Pevensy Park, past the brightly painted lodge cottage.

"Yes, it is," agreed Lavender. "If only it were not Porsche doing the training sessions."

"But Porsche is a brilliant rider," said her mother. "All the Pevensys are."

Lavender sighed. Her mother seemed incapable of reading between the lines when it came to human relationships. Thank goodness Aggie had taken her under her wing by getting her into committees. Lavender still suffered niggling worries that her mother wanted to replace her beloved Black Boy with a super-duper show pony. Being able to compete on Rapide in jumping events seemed to have distracted her mother from her original showing ambitions but recently Lavender had had a growth spurt, and this was obvious when she rode Black Boy and her legs hung down below the level of his tummy. Her mother wouldn't want to keep Black Boy just so Ruby had a pony to ride.

Some of the other Pony Club members had already arrived. With their matched pair of chestnuts, the Hennington brother and sister, Christopher and Catriona, were mounted and walking around the park looking at the jumps. Merry Barton, the third member of their team, was tacking up her mare Frolic.

"Good afternoon," she said coolly when Lavender and Ruby descended from the horsebox cab.

"Hello, your pony is looking very fit," said Lavender, desperately trying to think of an acceptable compliment. She could sense Merry's ill feelings emanating towards them. Merry gave her an unpleasant smug look and made no response. Lavender sighed. As three newcomers, Lettie, Ruby and herself were viewed with dark suspicion by the six pony club members who were the original Birtle teams.

"Don't worry about it," said Ruby in a voice loud enough to be heard by Merry. "Look! Here comes Lettie!"

"At least there are three of us," said Lavender quietly.

"What are you talking about, Lavender?" asked her mother loudly in her horrible pretentious accent.

"Mummy, please," pleaded Lavender, burying her face under Rapide's saddle flaps, doing up the girth.

Another horsebox trundled into the stable yard. The other team members were sitting in the seat behind the driver: Oswald Leadbetter, Jemima Grimsby, and Penelope Fletcher.

On the other side of the parking area, Lettie was unloading her pony, Cornish Boy. Her father's old Land Rover was hitched to a modest single-horse trailer, but Lettie looked very professional wearing a polo-necked green top and a pair of matching jodhpurs.

Within half an hour all the ponies were saddled, and the nine riders mounted and walked around.

"At least we have the advantage of having jumped these fences before," said Lavender, referring to the times that she and Ruby had ridden around the Pevensy Park cross-country course.

Lavender, Ruby and Lettie rode around together, and the six other riders were in a bunch, pointedly keeping some fifty yards away.

"We're definitely the outsiders," said Lettie with a wry grin.

Porsche, riding Diablo, and Susan King mounted on Troubadour appeared from the stable yard.

"Line up along here, everyone," called Susan.

The nine riders lined up their ponies, and were arranged into three teams.

"We'll do about thirty minutes schooling to warm up and then proceed to the jumps," announced Porsche. "Put your stirrups up to jumping length and trot around in a large circle."

The top team, the three chestnuts, followed each other, a carefully judged horse's length apart. They looked impressive, and competent, flashing around in their golden glory. They were followed by the second team. Oswald was an unpleasant-looking boy with a pallid complexion, large sticking-out ears and squinty little eyes. He had a whiney voice and was always complaining about how unfair things were. His brown pony, nondescript with a ewe neck, a long back and a triangular-shaped rump, skittered from one side to another. Lavender was fascinated, in a horrified way, by the double bridle. She had never seen anyone using one like this. The small bit was a twisted bridoon with a very sharp curb bit with long cheeks. To make this arrangement even more severe, he was using a very short running martingale attached to the top rein. She wondered whether such an arrangement was acceptable under pony club rules or whether Porsche would rule it out as too severe and recommend going back to basics and re-schooling the pony in a snaffle to improve its mouth.

Jemima Grimsby was riding a thickset cob that looked like he had spent his life jumping muddy ditches on the hunting field. He had an impressive Roman nose, legs as thick as kitchen table legs, and an enormous set of hindquarters. She was a wiry, drab-looking child with mousey hair, a pinched face, and a mouth twisted in a discontented line. To complete this team was Penelope Fletcher on a skewbald. He was not quite as cobby as Jemima's grey but had the same look about him, reliable but uninspiring and without the necessary speed needed to get fast times around a jumping course. Jemima was pudgy-faced with sallow skin.

Our team has to be better than Oswald's thought Lavender, feeling an unusual competitive rush. She didn't like the nasty, spiteful attitude of the other pony clubbers, and she would like to wipe those smug grins off their faces. Ruby had come across groups of children like this before, and she refused to let herself be intimidated. She was tougher than that. Lettie wasn't much interested in the vagaries of human behaviour. She was wrapped up in her pony and loved the companionship that she enjoyed with him. They were perfectly attuned to each other. She wasn't a people person. Naturally, she assumed that she would be picked for the regional finals. She had been the star of her pony club in Cornwall, and having won the junior open at Blossom Park, she was certain that she would be in the winning circle in Oxfordshire.

"That's enough trotting," said Porsche, obviously bored with the notion of ordinary schooling. "Form into your teams and canter on."

The three teams rode together in their respective groups. The trio of chestnuts cantered in perfect formation. Oswald's team didn't go well together. His pony rushed and veered around, and the two others stuck together in an uninspiring thudding canter.

"Put that brown pony in the middle of the other two," shouted Porsche. "Close in on him and keep him in line."

The skewbald and the grey weren't keen on getting too close to Oswald's brown pony, Jackdaw. It didn't really work.

Rapide, Cornish Boy and Black Boy kept their distance behind the others, cantering sedately in a neat bunch.

"Those three, the brown, grey and skewbald don't go well together," said Susan to Porsche, stating the obvious.

"I want to mix it up," said Porsche. "Oswald and Jackdaw, I want you with the two bays, and that black pony can go with the skewbald and grey."

"Oh no!" exclaimed Ruby. "I knew it! I knew it!"

There was nothing they could do.

Oswald peeled away from the two cobs and rode in between Cornish Boy and Rapide. They weren't keen on getting too close to the unhappy Jackdaw.

"Why have you got that bridle?" asked Lettie.

"Why do you think?" sneered Oswald. "He is very spirited, and I need it to control him."

"Then why can't you canter steadily in a circle?" persisted Lettie.

Oswald bared his teeth at her like a nasty dog threatening another in a back alley.

"Now, let's get down to some serious jumping," announced Porsche and rode towards the first jump, a brush that was four feet at one end, three feet six in the middle, and two feet six on the left-hand side. "I want you all to follow me," she said, cantering Diablo towards the high end.

"It's four feet," gasped Ruby, who had never jumped so high.

Susan determinedly followed Porsche, and Troubadour jumped the brush easily. The three chestnuts cantered towards the jump and cleared it in a single, synchronous leap. Next went Black Boy, the grey and the skewbald. Ruby lost her nerve at the last moment and swerved towards the lower end of the brush. Black Boy cleared the two-feet six-inch end, the other two also decided that four-feet was too high, and they jumped the three-feet-six side by side.

Rapide, Jackdaw and Cornish Boy were cantering together in a bunch. Lavender was worried that the long cheeks of Oswald's curb bit might get caught in one of their reins and bring them all down. They headed towards the high end of the brush fence and jumped it together. Rapide and Cornish Boy jumped high and wide, landing a length beyond Jackdaw, who had an ugly helicopter style of leaping.

"That was disgraceful," shouted Porsche in a fury.

"You three didn't do as you were told!" she raged, blazing at Ruby, Jemima and Penelope. They hung their heads in shame. "Oswald, you need to keep up with the others. Ride that pony properly!"

Lavender understood then that they were headed for disaster. Porsche seemed incapable of making helpful suggestions and thought that insulting and bullying people would make them do it properly. She didn't want to ride Rapide anywhere near the mad Jackdaw. She could see Ruby looking mulish with the other two.

"I don't think that the boy on his brown pony is a good match for my Cornish Boy," said Lettie, who was obviously not impressed by Porsche's aristocratic bloodlines, nor her schooling technique. "I'm not going to risk jumping with him." She turned and rode away back towards the stable yard where her father was waiting for her.

The others gasped. If Lettie can do it, so can I, thought Lavender. She turned Rapide and followed her new friend.

"Come on, Ruby," she called, slewing around in the saddle. Black Boy obediently trotted back with the others.

"I don't care about the regional finals," said Lettie. "It's not worth risking our ponies."

"I don't know what Aggie will say. You know that Rapide belongs to the Pevensys. It's very awkward, and Susan King is my mother's goddaughter and I'm caught up in the middle of other people's expectations."

"Tha' Porschey, she doan like me, at all," said Ruby.

They got back to the stable yard.

"Dad, I want to go home. I don't want to do this," said Lettie. Her father frowned at her but didn't question her in front of the others. They untacked Cornish Boy, loaded him and drove out within five minutes.

Ruby and Lavender looked at each other. Mrs E-H was still in the big house with Aggie. There was going to be some very awkward explanations to make. Eventually, Aggie and Lavender's mother came down to the stable yard.

"Just you two, where are the others?" asked Aggie.

"We don't think we're up to it," said Lavender, thinking this was more diplomatic than criticising the fearsome Porsche.

"But the three of you would have made a very good team," said Aggie in surprise.

"Lettie has taken Cornish Boy home. She doesn't want to enter anymore. She didn't want to jump him near the unreliable Jackdaw," explained Lavender.

"Jackdaw? Jackdaw?" queried Aggie.

"That Oswald's pony. He's brown, so Porsche thought he would go better with the two bays, but he's not very well-behaved. He's a bit erratic, and it got too hard," went on Lavender, thinking that it all sounded like a very weak-minded decision.

Aggie frowned.

"This is ridiculous, Lavender!" exclaimed her mother, thinking how embarrassing it was for her daughter to behave like this in front of the Duchess. "It was an honour to be picked for this special training. You can't just give up."

"Mummy, please," begged Lavender, feeling cornered. "Please, can we just go home and talk about it there."

Aggie saw that this situation had probably been created by Porsche, and she would deal with it better in private.

"They're upset, Evelyn. Perhaps you should take them home, and we'll talk about this later, just the two of us. I need to talk to Porsche."

"If you think that is best," said Evelyn, who never questioned Aggie's decisions. She would interrogate Lavender when they were alone, and Susan would know what had really happened.

They loaded the ponies and managed to leave Pevensy Park before the rest of them came back to the stable yard. Lavender sighed in relief, but she knew this was not the end of it.

Chapter Ten – Rapide is Taken Away

Porsche and Susan were conspiring against Ruby. When Aggie and Evelyn asked them what had happened at the coaching session, they blamed her. The story went that her action in taking the lower end of the jump had caused the others to rebel against Porsche's commands, and she was deemed too inexperienced to be up to jumping in a team. The worst of it was that Rapide was lent to Oswald until the regional finals so that he could ride him instead of the ill-trained Jackdaw. Aggie had explained to Evelyn that this was no reflection at all on Lavender's care of the pony, but for the sake of the honour of the pony club, they needed to enter the best possible teams.

Lavender and Ruby were devastated by this turn of events. There was now only one pony, and Mrs E-H insisted that for the next six weeks, Ruby wasn't needed, and Lavender and the gardener could care for Black Boy themselves.

"I don't care 'bout been paid or nuffin like that," pleaded Ruby, "an' it's too dark of an evening for you to ride after school, so I need to take Black Boy out."

"It's alright," said Lavender soothingly. "Of course, you can still ride Black Boy in the afternoon. But I'll muck him out in the morning, and the gardener can put him in the field at elevenses. I'm just worried he's going to be so lonely, separated from his best friend."

"Ponies 'ate been by themselves," said Ruby knowingly.

"It's only six weeks. At least that's what they say, but perhaps Aggie will decide not to send him back to us. What are we going to do?" moaned Lavender despairingly.

"It's that Porschey that's gone an dun this," said Ruby darkly. "We gotta fix 'er!"

"But look what happened last time. That's why she's so determined to get us back. It will only get worse if we go after her again," said Lavender, referring to the unfortunate incident when Ruby had dyed Porsche's horse Mangala green the night before the Blossom Park event.

The weeks after Rapide had left passed slowly. The nights drew in. It was dark when Lavender left for school and dark when she got back. Black Boy was sad, hanging his head disconsolately while he stood in the field.

"I don't want to go back to Pony Club after this," said Lavender to her mother.

"But dear, that's ridiculous. It's important for you to mix with other children of your own type," replied Mrs E-H. Susan had been in her ear about the undesirability of Ruby as a companion for Lavender. They had even arranged for Thea, the girl with the show pony, Summer Fancy, to come to tea. Mrs E-H insisted that Lavender would attend the next rally.

"It will be a chance for you to see how Rapide is getting on with that boy Oswald. Honestly, if you hadn't withdrawn from the selection, this would never have happened. You must think before you act so precipitously again."

Lavender knew that her mother was right. Even after Lettie had withdrawn from the selection, she could have hung on and perhaps been teamed with Penelope and Jemima, and Oswald and Jackdaw dropped. She tried not to think about that fateful coaching session. If only it had been Colonel Butterworth who had been training them and not Porsche.

Lavender went back to having lessons at Mrs Darcy's every Saturday. Things at the riding school had changed now that Mrs Darcy was back. Serena took the lessons with the more advanced riders. There were lots of new beginners, and they were being taught by Mrs Darcy, who had been circulating the neighbourhood drumming up business. There were a mob of youngsters who were second-generation students, their parents having been taught by Mrs Darcy when they were children.

The riding school had five new horses on full livery, and a new stable block was under construction. Business was booming. It seemed that everyone in Chatton, and many in Rychester, wanted to ride. Mrs Darcy's latest brain wave to increase the number of riding school ponies for all the new students was inspired by the novel *Six Ponies* by Josephine Pullein Thompson. She had purchased six unbroken New Forest ponies from a friend who lived on the edge of the forest. Then she designed a special course for the students that involved learning to break in ponies. It was very reasonably priced and included every aspect of the early handling and breaking-in process. It was the latest craze. The local Rychester newspaper had come out and taken some photos and was running a story.

Ruby had saved enough from her job as Lavender's groom to pay for herself to do the course. Serena had insisted that she had a hefty discount due to all the hours she had put in as an unpaid assistant. It was the first time Ruby was included in a group of students on equal terms and she was thriving. She had been chosen to be one of the first to sit on an unbroken pony and be led forward at the walk. She was bursting with enthusiasm for this new venture. It helped her to forget about losing her job looking after Black Boy and Rapide. She was not one to sit around in misery. She had more get up and go than that.

There was a pony club rally to be held one week before the regional final, and the teams were to jump in front of the other members, and the final selection would be made. Lavender was hoping that Oswald would fall off Rapide, and she would be put back on him and could make the team. Then she hated herself for wishing injury upon another human, even if it were the loathsome Oswald. She was astonished to see that Lettie had been persuaded to ride Cornish Boy in a team again. It felt like a sinister betrayal.

She and Thea sat on their ponies, watching the team riders jump around a course. Porsche had supervised the building of six sizeable jumps arranged in a circle around the field. It wasn't a proper cross-country course, but it was considered sufficient to test the ability of the ponies and riders.

The team of three chestnuts ridden by Christopher, Catriona and Merry cantered around together in perfect formation. Their horses' legs were synchronous, and they took off and landed without a misstep.

"They're sure to do well at the regional finals," said Thea.

"They deserve it," said Lavender, determined to be sporting.

The second team to be chosen was more interesting. There was Oswald on Rapide, Lettie on Cornish Boy, Jemima on her black cob, and Penelope on her skewbald pony. There were also two other contenders who had been co-opted at the last minute, a sixteen year old girl who rode a weedy thoroughbred with an upside-down neck and cow hocks, and a much younger girl, only ten years old who rode a fat pony with a determined rollicking canter.

They were sent off in pairs. Oswald and Lettie went first. Lavender winced as she watched Oswald's rough riding. Over every jump, he jabbed Rapide's mouth, and when he faltered at this treatment, Oswald kicked him roughly in the ribs. The next pair to jump were Jemima and Penelope. They trundled around, their ponies jumping carefully and correctly but without any dash or style. Then, Colonel Butterworth asked Lettie to have a go with the weedy thoroughbred. Surprisingly he jumped well, and Thea told Lavender that he had been an unsuccessful steeplechaser. Then, Jemima was teamed with the fat little pony with the young rider, but this was not so successful as the pony took two strides to every one of Jemima's pony, and they just couldn't keep together.

The girl on the weedy thoroughbred was called Hermione, Hermie for short, and her horse was called Roger. They were asked to jump around with Oswald and Lettie, and they went well. Hermie was a good rider, and she got the best out of Roger. They were declared to be the second team.

"I don't think I can bear to watch that Oswald riding Rapide," muttered Lavender.

"He doesn't have good hands," agreed Thea.

"Why was I so stupid to ride off and refuse to take part," moaned Lavender.

"We live and learn, as my mother would say," replied Thea. "Come on, it's lunch, and then we've got games this afternoon, which'll be fun. Mummy's not here today, so I think I might get away with some bending or musical poles."

"Black Boy is brill at that stuff," said Lavender.

They had fun that afternoon, and Thea and Summer Fancy were the overall champion bending combination.

"Fantastic!" said Lavender, congratulating her new friend.

"If only my mother would agree to me doing gymkhana games," moaned Thea.

"Mothers can be annoying," agreed Lavender.

"Are you going to watch the regional finals?" asked Thea.

"No, thank you very much. I don't think I could bear to watch poor Rapide being wrenched around. But to change the subject, did I tell you that I've got a puppy? I got him from the Miss Farthingtons, and he's adorable. I've called him Dollop. He's just a dollop of gorgeousness. It's the first dog we've ever had in my family, and it's making a big difference at home, it's kind of more homey."

"I know what you mean," said Thea. "My dog, Chippy, sleeps on my bed every night and keeps my feet warm."

"Mummy doesn't allow him in the bedrooms, nor the dining room when we're eating. At least he's got a basket near the range in the kitchen, so he stays warm. I've been training him to jump over a pole in the garden, and he's taken to it like a natural."

"Do you think Rapide will go back to your place after the regional finals?" asked Thea.

"I hope so. Even if he just goes back to Pevensy Park, he won't have Oswald riding him and ruining his mouth."

One week later, at the regional finals, the three chestnuts ridden by Christopher, Catriona and Merry came a very respectable third. The other team came nowhere. Rapide ran out at the second jump. This was very unusual behaviour for him. Aggie had been there to watch Oswald's riding style, and she had rung the stables and told Tom to bring the horsebox over immediately so she could rescue Rapide before more harm was done. She told Tom to take him to the Ellison-Heath's place.

Lavender heard the vehicle rumbling down the drive and ran outside. Seeing the Pevensy horsebox, she began to dance on the spot, flinging her legs and arms around like a demented marionette.

"Rapide! Rapide!" she called exuberantly.

He whinnied from inside the box.

"Well, he sounds glad to be back," said Tom as he lowered the ramp. "It's rare for a horse to react to someone's voice, not like he's a dog or anything."

"I can't wait to tell Ruby. She'll be so glad to be back to the old routine," said Lavender. "Mummy! Mummy! Look, it's Rapide! He's back!"

"There's no need to shout like that," said Mrs E-H, who had just had a phone call from Aggie.

Black Boy was running up and down the fence, whinnying at the top of his voice. Lavender led Rapide straight to the field so the two ponies could be reunited. They nuzzled each other and set off flying around the field, kicking out their hind legs with joy.

"We'll never let you two be separated again," said Lavender. Such a declaration was tempting the gods to practise their worst trick yet.

Chapter Eleven – Jill's Flying Visit

Just before Christmas, Jill Crewe stopped in Chatton for a few days. She had travelled from Porlock to Essex to pick up her chestnut mare, Copperplate. Now, she was on her way to her stepfather's Blainstock Castle in the Scottish Highlands. She had brought one of the other students with her, a rather quiet and serious German boy called Dieter.

"I've got tons to tell you," said Ann, almost babbling with excitement to have her beloved Jill back. Of course, Henry was wonderful, but talking to him wasn't the same as a good chin wag with Jill. Like twins, they finished each other's sentences. Henry had taken Dieter with him on his rounds, leaving Jill and Ann alone to catch up.

It would be harsh to label Ann a gossip. It would be more accurate to say that she took a great interest in her fellow human beings. She had not mentioned Susan King much in her letters to Jill. Although it was a fascinating topic, she had wanted to tell Jill face-to-face.

"I shall a tale unfold," said Ann with relish and unfolded it. "You know Susan Pyke, well, Susan King now. Remember I mentioned I came across her on the train and we were both going up to London so there was nothing for it but to talk to her and we ended up going around town together. It would have looked too strange to have ignored her when we were the only people in the carriage. Then we met up with Tartine, you remember my friend from Paris, and we bought outfits to go to dinner at the Pevensys."

"The Pevensys?" echoed Jill, trying to keep up with Ann's story being delivered in a breathless torrent.

"Yes, you must remember that girl Porsche who had Rapide at the hunter trials last year. Well, now Rapide has been passed down to the youngest girl, Morgan," said Ann impatiently.

"Yes, yes!" exclaimed Jill. "Lavender wrote to me and told me how Black Boy and Rapide found each other, and now they're back together again, and Rapide is staying at the Ellison-Heath's during term time."

"Yes, that's right. There's a very cute little gipsy girl called Ruby who has been riding Black Boy and helps look after them. They're both going to Birtle Pony Club now," ran on Ann. "But that's not the interesting bit . . . ."

Jill wondered when ponies had ceased to be interesting to Ann.

"It's Susan. She's got a terrific crush on one of the Pevensy young men, Austin. If it comes to anything, it will cause quite a stir."

"But Susan is married," said Jill, "she can't be chasing after another man."

"Oh, Jillikins! You can't be so naïve as all that," said Ann, looking at her friend in astonishment. "Don't you read the papers? They're full of divorces and all the sordid details."

"Do you think Susan will actually be divorced, and it will be reported in the newspaper?" asked Jill.

"I don't know that Susan's divorce will be in the paper. I don't even know if she will be divorced. I don't know that anything has actually happened. I think at the moment it is all in Susan's head. She's frightfully unhappy with Barty. We did always think he was a dull old stick in a young man's body. Anyway, there's more to it. The Pevensys persuaded Susan to swap that horrid black horse, Diablo and now Susan is swanning around on this absolute darling mare called Sassy Swoop."

"Oh!" said Jill, relieved that the subject had reverted to horses. "I never liked that Diablo. What is the new horse like?"

"It's a gorgeous dappled grey mare with long black lashes," said Ann. "It used to belong to Mercedes Pevensy, but she decided that the mare would never make it to the top, so now Susan has her."

"Would you say that you and Susan are friends now?" asked Jill, a tinny note in her voice, dismayed that perhaps she had lost her best friend to her childhood enemy.

"We see each other socially. The Pevensys do invite us over now and again. Henry went to school with Royce, and he is a good egg. Aggie, the Duchess, is something else. She's a force to be reckoned with. But the thing with Susan and Austin is that I think she really believes that somehow Barty is going to dissolve into thin air, and she's going to be waltzing down the aisle with Austin. Of course, it will never happen. Austin is a rackety young man with far too much charm and not an iota of commitment."

"Poor Susan," said Jill, genuinely feeling sorry for her erstwhile enemy. "I never would have thought that she would wander off the straight and narrow so dramatically. Who would have thought that the bright days of our youth would come to this? I'm glad that I've steered clear of all that palaver."

Ann looked at Jill with eyebrows raised. "But you can't imagine you're going to grow into an old maid surely? I was thinking that you're waiting for the right one to come along. What about Dieter?"

Jill looked at her friend in astonishment. Ann wondered if she had dropped some terrible brick.

"Oh, we're just chums. He's an orphan, you know, and a decent sort, but there's nothing romantic there," said Jill carelessly, shutting down the subject of any awkward entanglement in that direction. Ann was exasperated, but Jill adroitly changed the subject.

"How about you and Henry? Has he popped the question? We've been expecting a big announcement. It can't have gone off the boil?"

"Not at all," retorted Ann. "If I go to Bristol, then that's five years at university."

"If … Have you changed your mind?" asked Jill.

"It's just that I do love Chatton. I can't imagine leaving here for five whole years. I mean, I could marry Henry and settle down and help him with the veterinary work as a sort of assistant, and we could have half a dozen children," said Ann, voicing aloud, for the first time, her secret thoughts.

"I could see you with a brood of little pony clubbers," said Jill laughing.

"You're the one travelling the world and having adventures for the two of us. And I did go off to the Continent when Mummy was having me finished so I could eat an orange with a knife and fork," said Ann defensively.

"What does Henry say?" asked Jill curiously.

"I have only hinted at it. He doesn't say anything. I think he wants me to be sure in my mind without his two penn'orths," replied Ann. "He's amazing like that. He really respects me and wants me to make my own decisions."

"Obviously a paragon of every virtue," said Jill laughing.

"Now about going to London tomorrow, what's the plan?" asked Ann. They decided on a course of action for the following day's trip as Jill had to visit her literary agent, and they wanted to show Dieter the sights.

The few days that Jill spent in Chatton sped by, and the night before she and Dieter set off for Scotland, they had a dinner at Pool Cottage, just a cosy foursome – Ann, Henry, Jill and Dieter. Ann cooked one of her specialities, *boeuf en croute*, and they drank wine and made toasts late into the night. They went from the fate of nations to Skydiver and Jill's dressage career and also had a delightful reminisce about Dinah Dean, the strange girl who had upset the small community of Chatton as an errant child and was now a political force to be reckoned with at Cambridge where she was studying to become a lawyer.

Jill had wanted to go around to Lavender's to see Black Boy and Rapide, but she had run out of time. She resolved that the next time she came back to Chatton, it would be the first thing on her agenda.

Chapter Twelve – Wifely Virtues

As soon as Ann had waved goodbye to Jill and Dieter, she began to think about the bash being held at Pevensy Park on the Friday before Christmas. She was looking forward to it hugely. From what she had heard, it was always a fabulous affair. To be missed off the invitation list was considered social death. Just to show Henry that she could be frugal and not an expensive wife who had to have a new frock for every occasion, she planned to wear the gipsy dress that she had bought in London and had already worn on several occasions.

The prospect of the Pevensy party was making waves throughout the district. Whether one was invited or not became a point of honour. Of course, Susan King was invited, and also Barty and Susan's parents. The fact that Susan was married had become apparent to Aggie, and without comment, she had included Barty's name on the official invitation that was sent out. The Ellison-Heaths, Jessica and Felicia Farthington, Ann and Henry, the Bush family, and the Heath family. Mrs Darcy, Wendy Mead, Serena, Mr and Mrs Derry, Mrs Cholly-Sawcutt, and her three girls, Gary Horton, Mrs Whirtley and Dinah Dean, were also invited. Clarissa and her husband Charlie Morton were not, nor was Cecilia, Jill's cousin. Ruby and Lavender had been co-opted as helpers, and they were to circulate with Morgan offering platters of food to guests. Hired staff were to manage the drinks.

Susan had reluctantly told Barty about the invitation. There was no way of avoiding it. She had hoped that something might happen between her and Austin at the party but now that she had to drag along her boring husband, she feared her dreams would be crushed to dust and rubble. Susan's marriage was in a parlous state.

Barty pursed his lips and looked disapproving whenever she mentioned riding or competing, but she ignored him. She found everything he did annoying. From his habit of shaking out *The Times* over the breakfast table to the way he fussily placed his slippers in an exact position beside the bed every night. Once, she had waited until he was asleep and moved them two feet further down the bedroom floor so that when his feet were lowered, they would land on the carpet and not in the slippers.

Susan had realised with a painful jolt that she had signed her life away for a smothering, joyless existence, when just a hop, skip, and a jump could have taken her into a world full of promise and excitement. It wasn't even as if it were a life of dread and dark danger. It was humdrum and pointless.

What made it worse was that when reading Jill's young adult novels, she saw her once-despised classmate adventuring and discovering new worlds.

Jill was out there travelling, meeting all sorts of people, and she was stuck in Rychester, which was a town like a prim lady in white kid gloves. She was not sufficiently analytical to look into the core of Jill's being. Her erstwhile rival sought to improve herself, to be a better rider, a qualified instructor, also diligently practising her typing and shorthand, learning German and striking out into journalism, extending her writing skills beyond humorous autobiography. Susan knew that Jill was famous for having 'character' – what the heck did that mean? Everyone had a character!

Susan found herself shut in a prison of her own making. She was so unhappy and discontented that she wanted to smash her way out of her life, her marriage and the ghastly house on the newly built development. But she didn't make any rash moves. She had sufficient common sense to know that to leave her husband would render her position even more impossible. To have to scurry back to her parents' house would be abjectly humiliating, worse than staying married to Barty. She longed for Austin to rescue her. Sweep her into his arms and take her away so that she might share his charmed, golden life, and together they would breathe the wine-like air of pure romance.

Susan could not confide in any close friend, certainly not her mother! They might have pointed out the folly of such dreams, diagnosing her condition as the Falling for a Fairy Prince Complex. Why would Austin choose her from amongst the gaggle of girls that would be presented to him for his inspection? Girls who were not only well-bred, heiresses, suitable for a second son who would not inherit the title unless some accident resulted in the death of Royce, but also *single*.

She could not even remember her first meeting with Barty. It had been the idea of marriage, achieving marital status before her peers, that had inspired her to say yes to his proposal. She had not thought about virtues, such as honour, loyalty, charm and strength. Perhaps Barty did have a type of small honour, and he was certainly loyal to his firm. But charm and strength – none that she could discern. Now Austin had charm in bucket loads and was dashing and brave when it came to galloping over fences. She was seduced by Austin's glamour, and she felt herself adoring him and losing herself in the ocean depths.

Ann had inadvertently mentioned to her mother Susan's pash on Austin. It had bubbled out when they had been discussing who was going to the Christmas party and who wasn't. Mrs Derry was shocked by such a revelation. She was rather old-fashioned and fearful, a woman who thought that somehow worrying was protection against horrendous events. If you worried about it, then it meant it wouldn't happen.

After some serious thought, Mrs Derry felt compelled to go to Mrs Pyke, who was a fellow committee member of the Chatton Women's Institute. Over a cup of tea, in hushed tones, she communicated what Ann had told her. Mrs Pyke was deeply shocked. She had been more than satisfied with Susan's decision to marry Barty King. He was such a solid citizen, and the Pykes had been happy to see Susan settled so early while other parents waited anxiously to see how their daughters might fare in the marriage stakes. Becoming aware that all was not wonderful with Susan and her new husband, Mrs Pyke set out to discover if there was any truth in this unpleasant rumour. The thought that Susan would become the talk of the district was utter anathema to her. It was an enormous indiscretion and would follow Susan to the grave in such a small, close-knit community. Mrs Pyke had social aspirations based on sound morals. The Pykes prided themselves on their place in local society, but they were middle-class to the core. Even Jill's mother had been viewed as something of a bohemian as she made her living as a writer.

The day before the Pevensy Christmas bash, Mrs Pyke girded her loins to visit Susan, determined to have a serious mother-and-daughter talk. She had had an idea. She would bring up the subject in an oblique manner in the form of a book club discussion. She remembered reading *Little Women* as a girl and the way in which Mrs March had talked about the duties of wifedom to her eldest daughter, Meg.

Taking down her treasured volume, she searched for the relevant passage. It was in the chapter where Meg's marriage was going a little awry as she devoted herself to her twins. Obviously, devotion to one's babies was not in the same league as running around with irresponsible members of the aristocracy who got away with such behaviour due to their birth right.

Mrs Pyke put her copy of *Little Women* into her capacious handbag. The excuse for her visit was to give Susan some casserole dishes that were loitering at the back of one of her kitchen cupboards.

She arrived at the neat little house where Susan lived with Barty and thought how very satisfactory it was. It would be the envy of any young married couple. She remembered how she and her husband George had had to live with his parents when they had been first married during the war.

"Hullo Mother," said Susan, looking dishevelled in her dressing gown, her hair unbrushed and mascara smudges beneath her eyes.

Mrs Pyke was aghast at her daughter's appearance. She had hoped the whole story might have been an exaggeration, or even malicious gossip that had no basis in truth, but now she realised that all the signs were there. Her determination to be tactful dissolved in the face of Susan's unkempt appearance. She couldn't help but say, "Susan, were you expecting me?"

"Yes," replied Susan irritably.

"You're not dressed!"

"Well, you're my mother. You've certainly seen me in my dressing gown before," said Susan casually, looking into the distance. She decided then that as an adult in her own house, she might do as she liked and lit a cigarette.

Mrs Pyke bristled but sat there politely and waited, hoping that Susan might confide in her. She was strategic enough to know that she shouldn't launch straight into a homily about the proper behaviour of a good wife.

"How are things with you and Barty, darling?" she asked.

Susan shot her a dark look.

"Why do you ask?"

"I got the feeling that you might not be very happy with him at the moment," forged on Mrs Pyke. "You know darling, I was thinking about the little bumps in the road of early married life and it reminded me of some advice that I read in *Little Women*, when Mrs March talks to her eldest daughter Meg. I've marked the passage. Let me read it to you.

"Go out more, keep cheerful as well as busy, for you are the sunshine-maker of the family, and if you get dismal there is no fair weather."

"Now, what do you think? Doesn't that just sum it up beautifully? I think you should take an especial interest in Barty's work. It's something very important to him."

Susan looked at her mother in disbelief.

"The sunshine-maker! You have to be kidding! My view of marriage is that my husband should put himself out to make me happy!" she snapped.

"I think you've got to make an effort," said her mother helplessly, "you can't just give up on your marriage."

"I made a mistake. I should never have married him. It was a false start. Now, I know what real love is," declared Susan with an angry toss of her head.

"Real love!" gasped her mother. "Has Austin declared himself? Surely not!"

"Why not? Why shouldn't he love me?" raged Susan, not cottoning on to the fact that she hadn't mentioned Austin and wondering how her mother knew about him.

Mrs Pyke wasn't sure whether Austin had declared himself or not, but she dared not question her daughter further. It seemed that nothing but Austin's disinterest would drag Susan back from the brink of a very dangerous precipice. If she walked away from her marriage to be with Austin, who then did not come to the point of commitment, it would be an utter disaster. Even in these modern times, when divorce was more prevalent, it was still considered social death. The aristocracy might get away with such outrageous behaviour, but it was certainly not the done thing for the middle classes.

Susan stalked out of the room, down the hallway and through the front door, which she flung shut behind her with a satisfying bang. Standing on her front driveway, she realised she'd just walked out of her own home and was still wearing her dressing gown. So much for a dramatic exit! She was going to have to knock on the door and ask her mother to let her back in. Alternatively, she could wait until her mother was leaving and the door opened.

Old Mrs Dorian walked past with her shopping basket and looked at her curiously, her black eyes shining impudently. Susan found herself cowering on the porch, trying to take cover behind a shrub that was only half-grown. She was assailed with doubts brought on by her mother's speech. Was she fooling herself about Austin? Did he love her? How had she taken such a wrong course in her life? She whimpered like a beaten dog and wished that she could go away and not step foot in Oxfordshire again. Perhaps she should go to Africa and become a missionary.

Eventually, Mrs Pyke opened the front door. She had been waiting for Susan to return but had given up. Susan slunk back through the door, went into the living room, and melodramatically threw herself down on the sofa.

"Susan, what on earth has got into you?" asked her mother. "This isn't like you at all!"

"I hate Barty! He's horrible!" she declared. "And right now, I want to be alone!"

"That's very Greta Garbo of you!" exclaimed Mrs Pyke. "I'll leave you then. Presumably, we'll see you *and Barty* at the party tomorrow night. Please don't make a fool of yourself, dear. We've lived here all our lives, and as Pykes, we hold our heads up high. I couldn't bear it if we became a laughing stock."

Susan buried her head into a satin cushion. All her mother cared about was what other people thought. She didn't care at all about her only daughter's happiness.

Chapter Thirteen – The Christmas Party

"Deck the halls with boughs of holly, da da da de da!" sang Morgan, Lavender and Ruby raucously. They were rushing around the banqueting hall pinning up swathes of brightly coloured plaited ribbons and big bunches of greenery that the gardeners had brought in. A giant Christmas tree had been placed in the corner of the hall, and small presents for the children were hanging from every branch. They were to be handed out by the Duke early in the evening.

"Shut up with that racket!" shouted Porsche at them, her face black as thunder.

"No Christmas spirit for you!" snapped Morgan at her. "The evil fairy will bring you bad luck and a lump of coal in your stocking!"

"Having you as a brat of a sister is bad luck enough!" retorted Porsche. "Not to mention your little goblin friends!"

The ill-feeling between the younger girls and Porsche had not dissipated.

"Girls, girls, I want you to put fresh flowers in all the guest rooms. We'll be full to the gunnels tonight," commanded Aggie like a major general.

"Porsche, I want you to dash down to the village shop for nutmeg. Cook says we've run out."

"How many people have you invited to this gala?" asked Louis, making a rare appearance on the scene.

"Oh, hundreds!" replied Aggie cheerily. "Each of the children has invited their friends. I think Mercedes alone has issued invitations to every single three-day eventer in England. With the Tokyo Olympics coming up next year, there is a lot of excitement in the ranks, from the lowest to the top echelons of the sport. Even those who have no chance at all of being included in the long list for the British team are buzzing around speculating, flattering those with any pull and backstabbing their best friends. They should all be here tonight. Every bed is going to be filled and we've got people staying in all the big houses in the county and the local hostelries are booked out."

The Pevensy family gathered in the hall and were sipping champagne when the first guests began to arrive. Porsche was turned out to shock. Ann might consider herself rather up to the minute with her geometric-designed short dresses, long boots, and gipsy outfits, but in contrast, she was merely soft-pedalling Kings Road chic. Porsche adopted a different look, inspired by the hip, beatnik artistic community in London. She was wearing Max Factor pancake, black eyeliner, white lipstick, lacy black stockings, the most mini of mini-skirts, and almond-toed Cossack boots with Louis heels. This was hardline, counter-culture, but perhaps merely token rebellion.

Cars swept down the circular drive, and the guests tumbled up the steps to be greeted by Aggie and Louis. Their vehicles were taken away by the gardeners and men from Shrove Langton and parked in a large flat area in the park. The band from London was set up at the end of the banqueting hall. They were all dressed in pale lavender, which had the effect of making the stouter members look like well-tailored cushions. They were playing jazzed-up versions of popular Christmas songs. The smell of sweet cinnamon, nutmeg, hot mince pies and brandy butter pervaded the air. Huge fires were blazing and crackling in all the fireplaces, apple tree logs giving off a pleasant smell.

The local county had turned up in force, decked out in formal evening dress. The women wore long gloves, and some even sported tiaras that sparkled in their carefully coiffed hair. There was a proliferation of green, red and tartan materials and through the air swirled a mixture of heavy, cloying perfumes. Children of all ages were clustered around the Christmas tree, speculating on the different-sized packages that were marked with gender and age group suitability. They were chattering away and grabbing up the small, savoury sausage rolls that Morgan carried around on a large silver platter.

"No more than two each," she instructed.

Ruby came up with the mince pies, each topped with a dollop of brandy cream.

"Hope this brandy doan go to yer 'eads," she quipped.

They all laughed and giggled.

"Would you like me to help you carry around some food?" asked Thea, who had just arrived with her parents.

"That would be helpful," said Morgan, "If you go through the banqueting hall, you'll find Cook with the platters in the room beyond.

Susan King arrived with Barty and found it almost impossible to keep her face straight when confronted by Porsche in her bizarre outfit. She managed to achieve a semblance of cool and kissed her new best friend on both cheeks. She and Porsche went over and stood in the corner of the hall, laughing over secret bitchy comments about the other guests. Barty was left to find himself someone to talk to and hurried over to some of the older gentlemen who began to pump him for free legal advice. Mrs Whirtley and Mrs Darcy were exchanging news in their booming voices, and Dinah Dean was lecturing a group of earnest young women who took world affairs very seriously. The two Miss Farthingtons were having a chat with Wendy Mead and Serena, probably discussing Patchwork's progress. April Cholly-Sawcutt had her hand clamped around Gary's arm, not allowing him to wander off and talk to any of the glamorous young women who were circulating with calculating eyes, looking for potential beaux.

James Bush was following Mercedes with his eyes, ready to move to engage her in conversation. Diana Bush was laughing with Mr and Mrs Heath. Jackie stood there silently, looking left out. Mrs Derry had her head together with Mrs Pyke, who was looking worried, casting anxious glances towards her daughter.

Royce had gathered together a clan of close friends from his Oxford days who had all belonged to a secret society of poets. Louis was introducing his chums, who were ardent car enthusiasts, to some of the local people.

"Goodness! Who is that girl over there?" Ann asked Henry in an amazed accent. "She has practically every man in the room buzzing around her like bees swarming the most divine flower. She looks like a delicate angel!"

Henry laughed heartily. "Yes, she is attracting a great deal of attention. The *on dit* is that she is the daughter of the new vicar at St Augustine's in Oxford. A lot of the male students have suddenly started attending morning service."

"A vicar's daughter!" exclaimed Ann. "Whatever next? I wouldn't have thought it with that dress. She is decidedly underclad. She looks so delicate it's a wonder she can stand up to such a rush of attention."

"You see, she makes a chap want to take care of her," explained Henry. "As if she should always be dressed in white lace and kept in a box, and you want to take her out just to look at her."

Ann thought about this seriously for a minute or two. She admired the fresh, youthful beauty of the young woman, the slight figure, the guileless eyes, the carnation-pink blush on her perfectly-planed cheeks, and the tender, unsure curve of her lips that falsely denoted the artlessness of her character.

"Do you want to go over and join the throng?" Ann asked Henry in a voice remarkably free from suspicion and spite.

"No, my darling. I want you by my side to help me pull a calf out of a cow when it gets stuck."

Ann laughed merrily. "Well, thank goodness for that! But you know I'm curious to meet her. I rather like the idea of making the acquaintance of someone so unlike Jill and myself, with our boisterous good spirits and up for anything attitude. You stay here, and I'll be back shortly. You can mingle with the crowd around Dinah Dean and tell me the latest line of thought in radical politics."

Ann made her way over to the crowd of admirers.

"Hello darling," she said to Royce, who was mooning over the girl from the outer circle. Her elfin charm probably appeals to his poetic nature, thought Ann. "Do introduce me to this charming young girl."

"Of course," said Royce assiduously, polite to the core of his being.

"Seraphina, may I introduce you to Ann Derry. She is a Chattonite of the first order, and has lived here all her life."

"Delighted to make your acquaintance," said Seraphina in a tiny, breathless voice. She extended a soft, warm hand, and Ann took it, thinking that it felt as limp as a recently deceased mouse. She couldn't help giggling.

"You have acquired a gaggle of admirers," observed Ann.

"Oh, do you think so," said Seraphina artlessly, as if the thought had never occurred to her.

Ann hung around for a few minutes and then made her way back to Henry.

"Do you think she would make a good Duchess?" she whispered to him, in the matter-of-fact tones of one who might run a marriage bureau. "I do think that Royce is struck on her."

"I'm not sure that there is one type for a Duchess, not in these modern times," said Henry thoughtfully.

"You're quite right," replied Ann blushing at the snobbishness of her stereotypical view. "Aggie is such a type. She is the only Duchess I have ever met, so I am influenced by her."

"Royce is quite similar to his father, you know," said Henry. "Louis is rather shy, retiring and diffident, and he chose a woman who can take charge, and he chugs along in her wake. Royce is quiet and unassuming, but he has fallen very hard for this china doll girl, I believe."

"He seems to be the most eligible of that bunch of ardent suitors," said Ann.

"Perhaps being a potential Duke will stand him in good stead," replied Henry. "And he is a faithful, steady sort of a chap. You know that fellow with the longish hair that flops over his forehead, he is a Marquis, I believe."

"Really, I did miss out. I should have shone some of my earthy charm upon him," said Ann with a mischievous gleam in her eye. She was surveying the room and spotted Austin entertaining a bunch of giggling young women.

"Well, if Royce is a sensitive gentlemanlike man, it is certainly more than you can say for Austin," she commented. "I never thought I would say this, but poor Susan is being led a merry dance, I fear."

"Austin is a player of the first order, his behaviour is caddish" said Henry disapprovingly.

"You're quite right, and to think I thought he might be suitable for Jill. What on earth was I thinking!" cried Ann, throwing her hand melodramatically to her forehead.

There was a commotion at the front door, and a large contingent of people pressed in, streaming through the foyer and into the banqueting hall. The drinks staff converged on them with champagne and various other tipples. It was the three-day event crowd. The locals broke off from their conversations and stared with open mouths at these people, many of whom they only recognised from photos in *Horse and Hound* and interviews on the television sports programmes.

"Oh, my goodness! Jumping Russian rabbits! There's the Bulstrode sisters!" cried Ann.

James Bush, who had been holding forth to a small crowd of locals, looked over at the pair of sisters. The eldest Laura was famous in showing circles and was now rising to the top of the dressage ranks, such as they were in England. The younger sister, Janet, worked as a nurse but managed to ride in numerous horse trials. He wondered whether he shouldn't exert his charms in that direction rather than Mercedes.

"There's Mark Lansdowne! You know Jill's stepfather's nephew. I met him when I was up in Scotland. He's with his girlfriend, Diana Barton-Tompkin," whispered Ann in Henry's ear.

"Well, if his girlfriend is Diana whatever-whatever, why is he standing there as if struck by lightning staring at Mercedes Pevensy?" asked Henry.

"He is being rather obvious, don't you think? I thought he had more *savoir-faire*."

"Look! He's heading for Mercedes now. The girlfriend is looking rather grim," commented Henry.

As regular readers would know, Mark Lansdowne has had a starring role as a 'baddie' in many of the previous Jill books. He had effortlessly made an enemy of Jill Crewe when she had arrived at Blainstock Castle two years ago. He was arrogant with an unattractive giant-sized chip on his shoulder about the fact that he was the second-born and his elder brother, Horatio, would inherit the sizeable Lansdowne estate, which was situated next to

Blainstock Castle. He had had hopes that he might inherit Jill's step father, Richard Micheldever's estate, but now all chance of that was dashed as Richard, having married Jill's mother, had an infant son, Hamish.

Mark was ambitious and determined but still struggling to rise to the top of the three-day eventing world. He was undoubtedly a good rider but had a tendency to be rough and dominant, rather than persuasive with his horses, taking shortcuts in their training. He and Diana Barton-Tompkin had been an item for several years now. He had been staying at her family home in Yorkshire during the summer, keeping some of his horses there, leaving others in the care of the Blainstock stable staff in Scotland. Diana was an icy-blue-eyed society beauty, famous for her wit and heartlessness, who regularly contributed nasty, gossipy items to one of the more scurrilous tabloid newspapers.

Behaving in an uncharacteristically uncool manner, Mark left Diana to her own devices and rushed over and introduced himself to Mercedes, who was impeccably polite but showed no special interest in him. She had seen him around at events but never talked to him before. Then, the Miss Farthingtons hurried over.

"Mercedes, dear, we've just been talking about Patchwork and his training. We thought he might be ready to enter some one-day events in the spring. We wondered if you could suggest which first event we might try him out at?" said Jessica.

Mark was annoyed at these two eccentric old women interrupting his first conversation with Mercedes. He felt as if he had been struck by lightning, and he was entranced by her cool, perfect beauty. Instinctively, he wanted her all to himself.

"I'm sorry we're interrupting you," said Jessica.

"Not at all. Let me introduce you. Jessica and Felicia Farthington, this is Mark. ." for a moment, Mercedes struggled to remember his surname, then it came to her, "Lansdowne."

"How do you do."

"How do you do."

How do you do."

"Mark is also a three-day eventer. Perhaps you could suggest a possible event, preferably in Oxfordshire or nearby, that would suit a promising young novice?" suggested Mercedes.

Mark was irritated at the interruption. Then, to his dismay, he saw that Mercedes was using it as an excuse to drift away. He was left with these two tattered old women. They were looking him over appraisingly, noticing his taut, trim physique.

"Mark Lansdowne, I'm sure I've seen your face in *Horse and Hound*," said Jessica, who read every copy with great attention.

"Do you live around here?" asked Felicia.

"I'm based up in Scotland, and I've been staying in Yorkshire over the summer," replied Mark.

"What a shame. If you were local, you could perhaps come and try out our Patchwork," said Jessica. "We've got a local girl from the riding school training him. We were going to ask Mercedes if we could take him over to Pevensy Park and give him a spin around their cross-country course. It would be interesting to see how he would go for a man."

"Well," said Mark, an idea springing into his mind, "there is a chance I might be down in Oxfordshire for a while. I would be happy to come over and give him a twirl over the jumps. Has he competed at all yet?"

"He did a very creditable round at Blossom Park Hunter Trials this year. Then he's been doing flatwork for some months now. We think he is ready to enter a one-day event. It would be good if you could advise us," said Felicia, who had taken a liking to this dashingly handsome young man. "Why don't you come and stay with us? Bring your horses with you. You would be very welcome."

"That's very kind of you," said Mark, not even trying to hide the insincerity in his voice.

"We would love to have you stay," said Felicia breathlessly. Jessica frowned and nodded her head like a sparrow. She wasn't sure that their house was up to entertaining such a handsome young man. But there was no stopping Felicia when she got an idea into her head. "There is room for your horses, and there is a lot going on around here."

Mark's hooked nostrils curled. He scented advantage to himself. These old women seemed harmless enough, and he was fascinated by Mercedes, who had so coolly spoken to him then drifted on as if he was of no account. He was determined that he must get to know her better.

"How did you come by this horse?" he asked.

"Well, that is a story," replied Felicia happily.

Mark thought to himself, of course, undoubtedly a long and extremely dull story, but he arranged his face in an interested expression.

"We have a variety of animals at our place. We like to think of it as a refuge for the rejected and unwanted. One of our friends found him pulling a cart through the East End of London and bought him and put him on a train to Oxford. He's been here for twelve months now," explained Jessica.

A groan almost escaped through Mark's thin lips. A beaten-up carthorse did not sound promising.

"I tell you what. You give me your address and phone number, and I'll contact you when I'm coming down, perhaps just a week or so after New Year.

"Oh, that would be smashing," enthused Felicia. "We would love to have you come and stay. A big strong chap like yourself."

Mark imagined that he might be put to work helping to build enclosures for all the rescues. The thought was frightful, but he was determined to pursue Mercedes, and this seemed as good a way as any other. He didn't pause to reflect that this was out of character for himself. He had known many beautiful women in his life. He had been pursued by several society beauties.

As Mercedes walked across the room, it was as if she were moving along a golden path. Everyone turned and looked at her. It wasn't just beauty, but something more than that. Tolerance and generosity seemed to emanate from her. Mark imagined that she cast a theatrical light, so that to see anything through her eyes was to see it in brighter colours. Her cloud of dark hair was a halo, and her wide, generous curving mouth hinted at an inner beauty that he had never seen in any other woman. Previously, he had liked to watch admiration of himself in women's eyes, like Narcissus looking in the pool at his reflection of handsome manhood. But this was different.

He was so caught up in this wondrous vision that he quite forgot Diana. She was seething. She had never seen Mark looking so gormless. She was not going to put up with this. It was entirely unacceptable. She flounced off, feeling utterly humiliated. Mark being lovestruck was something that she had never seen before. On her way out of the room, she ran into Eddie Hatton. She had known him for years. In their youth, they had run in the same set.

"Di! You look gorgeous, as usual!" he brayed.

"Oh, Eddie! This place is such a bore. Full of horsey types. Take me away!" she cried melodramatically.

Eddie was one of the few non-horsey people at the party. He had always adored Diana and now found himself in the enviable position of being her knight in shining armour.

"But Mark?"

"Never mind about Mark, let's go!"

He took her arm and led her chivalrously out through the front door to his natty little sports car. In several minutes they were through the gate and speeding away.

The floor was clear in the middle of the banqueting hall. It was time for dancing. The band played a Viennese waltz. The guests who liked to dance were swirling around like leaves dancing on a rapid stream. The band played on and on with a sense of speed and rhythm, Ann and Henry put up a reasonable show. Louis danced with Mercedes. Aggie with Colonel Butterworth. Mr and Mrs Derry, Mr and Mrs Bush, Mrs Darcy and James Bush, Royce and Serafina all paired up together.

Mark was desperate to dance with Mercedes and stood on the sidelines. He did not notice that Diana had left. In the same way, that he was determined to win, to ride for Britain, he wanted Mercedes. She was the ultimate prize. He swore to himself that he would never look at another woman. This was an overwhelming desire for possession, an unerasable printing of her face on his brain. He knew that she would haunt his memory every day of his life if he did not possess her. His life had become simplified, focused on one point. Everything else was unworthy of even a moment's attention.

Susan and Porsche stood awkwardly in the corner. Susan was dreading that Barty might reappear and she would be forced to dance with him. Porsche had no desire to dance at all.

"Good evening," said Austin, bowling up to them. "May I ask you to dance, Mademoiselle?" he said, bowing in front of Susan. She went bright pink, and in a trice, he had whirled her onto the dance floor, and she was in his arms. Absolute bliss!

Susan was in such an infatuated daze that she wasn't thinking clearly. She didn't realise that Austin had a penchant for married women. She had assumed that when he discovered she was married that he would lose all interest. She didn't really understand him at all. He not only enjoyed the feeling that he was stealing a march on some hapless husband, but he was less likely to find himself in a tight corner with a young maiden demanding that he marry her.

"Would you like to take a turn about the garden with me?" he asked. She nodded at him, unable to get a single word past her lips. He led her to the side of the hall, and they slipped through a small discreet door, down a short corridor and out into the garden at the side of the house.

A bright moon shone in a sky full of racing clouds. The shadows of trees and hedges cast soft mysterious pools of darkness on the lawn. He led her by the hand to a small topiary garden. Her clinging dress was illuminated by a glittering wash of moonlight, and her eyes were sparkling like stars as she followed in his wake.

There was a love seat nestled between the hedge plants that were sculpted as bizarre birds.

He drew her into his arms and kissed her on the lips. Susan thought she was in paradise. She was overcome with a sensation of music playing, jewels flashing, and liquid gold for blood in her veins.

"Oh, you are the most divine woman," sighed Austin ecstatically.

Susan desperately wanted to be cool, elegant, hard as a diamond, just like Mercedes. Instead, she found herself bending to his will like a goldfish-girl snapping up ants' eggs on the brimming surface of life. She couldn't resist. She swooned in his arms, overcome with thrilling fervour.

Afterwards, they slipped back to the party, and Austin said he would go in ahead of her and she should follow in a minute or two. The band was playing a lively waltz, and the dance floor was full of couples whizzing around. Susan sidled in, feeling as if everyone there would know what had occurred. She stood for a moment in the dark shadow of the alcove. No one seemed to be looking her way, and she made her way as casually as she could around the edge of the room, looking for a member of staff carrying a tray of drinks.

"Susan! There you are! I've been looking for you everywhere," said Barty.

She stared at him helplessly, like a rabbit caught in the headlights.

"Come on, let's dance. We must have at least one turn about the dance floor. I've been partnered with three different matrons, doing my duty, and now I want to dance with my wife."

She nodded acquiescence. This was as gallant as Barty ever got. She was utterly cast down. At the same moment, Austin swept by with one of those dainty, modern misses from Oxford who had arrived fashionably late with a bunch of his college friends.

The music played on. Susan didn't know what to think. Was Austin amusing himself at her expense, or was he truly struck on her? She had so little experience of men and the world of romance and dalliance. She noticed her mother watching her suspiciously. Perhaps she had seen her slip away with Austin? She dreaded to think what homilies her mother might deliver at their next morning tea. The everyday world was closing in around her and all sense of magical romance dissipated as she listened to Barty droning on about the conversations he had had that evening.

The last of the party goers dispersed at three in the morning. The banqueting hall was left in disarray, tinsel and streamers were hanging forlornly, empty plates and glasses lay scattered in odd corners of the room, the Christmas tree had lost its glamour now all the small, delectable presents had been given away, and the wooden floor was scuffed and scattered with crumbs and dirt.

Chapter Fourteen – Mark Arrives in Oxfordshire

Mark Lansdowne had gone home to Scotland for Christmas. It was then that he heard the devastating news that his family's trust fund had been plundered. His generous income, which had funded his competition career, had disappeared over the horizon, stolen by a crooked lawyer. He had no personal savings, and for the first time in his life, he was going to have to pay his own way.

Early in the New Year he loaded two of his horses in his huge horsebox and drove to Oxfordshire. He was determined to pursue Mercedes. He was experiencing an unusual boiling-over *bouillabaisse* of emotions. He was certain she was 'the one' – the epitome of any horseman's dreams. Not only was she divinely beautiful, with perfectly cast features and a peach-tinged flawless complexion, but she also had an irresistible air of untouchability. As far as he could ascertain, she had never dated anyone, totally dedicated to her horses and her equestrian career. Her best friend seemed to be her very ambitious mother. Another advantage, now of crucial importance, was that her family was extremely wealthy!

When Mark had first thought to go to Oxfordshire, he had certainly not planned to stay with the Farthingtons. He had been prepared to humour them by riding their horse around a bit, but had imagined that he would set himself up in one of the well-known yards there. His first thought had been the Cholly-Sawcutts, who had several high-performing horses belonging to well-known riders on livery. The yard certainly had good showjumping facilities, and he hoped that he might have access to the Pevensy Park cross-country course. He wasn't keen on Gary Horton, who seemed to be an extremely self-satisfied individual. Mark's introspective abilities were not finely honed enough to see that he and Gary Horton were cut from the same cloth!

There was now no way that he could afford the very high livery fees charged by the Cholly-Sawcutts. He could not even afford Mrs Darcy's much more reasonable fees. At the Pevensy Christmas party, the Farthingtons had suggested that he stay with them, and he had laughed to himself at such a ludicrous offer. Now, it seemed that it was his only option, free accommodation and the obligation to ride a half-trained horse – a skewbald of all things! He had wrongly imagined that there would be stable staff and some reasonable facilities. But, still, he felt as if he were plummeting to the depths of financial degradation.

The weather was suitably dramatic as he turned his juggernaut of a horsebox through the Farthingtons' front gates. Lightning was racing up and down the sky and lit up the face of the house, which looked Gothic.

Swirling gusts of wind grabbed him and almost threw him off balance as he descended from the driving seat in the only place to park which was on the overgrown gravel in front of the house entrance. To get out again, he was going to have to reverse through the gates. He had been annoyed that the road to the stable yard was not clearly signed.

Felicia and Jessica were standing on the porch fluttering with excitement that this handsome young man was really coming to live with them. Mark hoped that it was only going to be temporary and that he might be invited to stay at Pevensy Park, but he had to step carefully in his courtship of Mercedes. This would be a useful billet until he pulled it off.

He rushed up the stairs, across the porch, and they ushered him into the hall. Even such a short sprint in the pouring rain left him dripping onto the floor. He shook himself like a dog.

Jessica and Felicia took him into the drawing room. He was dismayed to see the condition of the interior of the house. Rain was slamming and beating against the uncurtained windows, and the noise seemed to drive home the dawning truth.

They offered him tea and sandwiches. He sipped from a cup of tea that was sitting on a mismatched saucer. Starving, he helped himself to several sandwiches. Imagine his distaste when he found not one but half a dozen hairs in the fish paste filling. His stock of good manners was now at its limit. A disreputable tomcat, with ears like punched train tickets and a tail chewed to a string, was staring at him with slanted green eyes set in a pugilist's face. Jessica absent-mindedly stroked him, and he purred rustily. Mark felt as if the tattered animal were challenging him, one male to another.

"I've to get the horses settled. It's been a long journey for them. Perhaps you could take me over or direct me to the stables, and I can make sure they're set up," asked Mark, putting down his plate of not even half-eaten sandwiches.

"Oh," said Felicia. "I thought you might already know. I thought everyone knew. It's the talk of the village . . . our arrangements."

Mark looked out the window, and a sheet of lightning lit up the landscape. He could see a line of beeches tossing at the bottom of the meadow. The black hills beyond were outlined as if by a steel pen etched against the dark sky.

"I have no idea what you're talking about," he replied shortly.

"We'll show you where we keep Patchwork. We thought you might put your horses in with him. It is quite a spacious area."

Mark imagined some sort of barn where the horses might roam free. He frowned. There was no way his precious horses were going to be rubbing shoulders with this Patchwork.

The Farthingtons went to the door, and he followed them. Can you imagine his surprise when they led him down a crowded passageway, thick with the smell of puppies, and into the dining room where Patchwork was munching his bucket of feed in solitary splendour beneath the crystal chandelier?

At the core of his being, Mark was deeply conventional, having been raised by a stern and conservative father who was by nature militaristic. 'Imaginative' was certainly not Mark's middle name. He had never even considered such an arrangement. He found it impossible to hide his astonishment and horror. Felicia and Jessica might live with their heads in the clouds, but they could not fail to notice Mark's reaction.

"If you didn't want them to roam around together, then perhaps we could partition the room?" suggested Jessica timidly.

There were several minutes of deadly silence. Mark was utterly appalled. What on earth was happening to him? The family losing their money had been bad enough, but it was, at least, the sort of thing that happened to the best of people. This was ludicrous. Apparently, everyone in the area knew. The Pevensys would certainly know about this arrangement, and he was about to become the local joke. Jill Crewe came from Chatton, and he shuddered with the knowledge that she would be fully aware of his plunge into utter ridiculousness.

He thought about his two horses in the horsebox. He had brought British Brown, on whom he had been competing for the last three years. He had taken him to Burghley and Badminton with no placings but finishing respectably in the middle of the field. He had planned on trying to sell him as a reliable and experienced eventer in the spring, giving him some cash to keep going. He needed money to be able to wine and dine Mercedes if he were to make any headway in that direction.

The other horse was an extremely handsome big grey, Kilkarny King, still a novice, who had competed very creditably in several one-day events and was ready to step up to three-day events in the coming season. Most of Mark's hopes rested on him, and there was no way he would let some skewbald mongrel kick and injure him in this ridiculous setup. He was beyond looking at Patchwork to see what he thought of him. Fury was stirring in his soul, and he very nearly exploded in the face of the poor Farthingtons, who were wringing their hands in despair at his reaction to their arrangements.

Finally, Mark managed to utter in a tightly controlled voice, "I'll leave the two horses in the horse box, and arrange the partitions, so they have room to move about. Perhaps we can do something about partitions in here tomorrow. Do you have any outbuildings that could be used as stables?"

"We do have the old stables, but the roof is hopeless. It needs to be completely replaced. You can look around, but there really are no suitable outbuildings for horses," admitted Felicia.

At this, Mark turned on his heel and climbed into the back of the horsebox. Brownie, as he called British Brown, and King were restless, weary from their long journey. He re-arranged the partitions, so each of them had half of the enormous horsebox to walk around in. It could travel with eight horses, so they each had a space larger than an old-fashioned stall but smaller than a regular loose box. Mark measured out their feeds, giving them a generous ration of horse nuts, which had just come onto the market and were all the rage in the world of horse comestibles.

He couldn't bear to go back into the house. He was beyond caring about even the appearance of politeness. He sat down in the sleeping area of the truck. He found what was left of a packet of sandwiches that his parents' cook had prepared for him and drank straight from a whisky bottle until he reached a comatose state and lay down on the bunk fully clothed and sank into unconsciousness.

The following morning Mark woke in a black mood. Knowledge of his present uncomfortable position rushed in and swamped his consciousness. He groaned, turned over and shut his eyes. Perhaps it had been a nightmare, and he would wake up in his comfortable bed in the family home in Scotland.

"Mark!" called one of the Farthingtons outside the truck. "I've brought you a cup of tea."

He groaned and swore softly under his breath. To be attended by the old ladies was somehow insulting to his manhood. He opened the personnel door.

"Good morning!" said Felicia brightly.

"Good morning," he replied grumpily. There was nothing good about it!

"Would you like some help with your horses? We're so interested to see them," said Felicia, hanging around while he sipped on the cup of tea, which was weak with too much sugar.

"I can manage," he muttered impolitely. His manners had deserted him.

"Mercedes has rung up. She says she is coming over this morning," continued Felicia.

Mark's heart jolted, his brain slid into gear, and adrenalin began to pump around his body. He was mortified that his future love would see him in such an ignominious position.

"Is it possible to use your bathroom to freshen up," he asked, rubbing his bristly chin.

"But of course. We expected you to sleep in the bedroom, and there is a bathroom right next door for your exclusive use," said Felicia. She spoke as if they were providing hotel accommodation, with furniture upholstered in woven fabrics, taffeta, gilt-edged and marble.

"I'll go up now and get dressed, and then I'll be back down to sort out the horses. Do you have a field where we can park them?" he asked.

"There is a bit of a paddock out the back where we let out Patchwork during the day. They can all go in there together. Patchwork will enjoy the company," Felicia replied as if their gelding's well-being was the highest priority.

Mark bounded up the front steps of the house and waited impatiently for Felicia to totter after him to show him the way to the bathroom. The doggy smell was all-pervasive. He couldn't believe that he had sunk to such depths. If only Mercedes would take pity on him and insist that he move to Pevensy Park immediately.

Ten minutes later, he descended the steps, freshly shaven with cold water as the hot water system didn't work. He had changed into a clean shirt and breeches. Mercedes drove up to the front entrance in a shiny, posh saloon car. She stepped out into the winter sunlight, and he remembered just how divinely beautiful she was. His heart filled with longing. She immediately offered to help him unload the horses, and he was ashamed for her to see how they had spent the night in such mucky conditions. He was hardly presenting himself in a good light.

"We're going to Tiddington Hunter Trials next week," said Mercedes. "Perhaps you could take your horses, as well. They certainly look fit."

"That sounds good," said Mark, eager to prove himself, and Tiddington was as good a venue as any.

"You could bring your horses over to our place to give them a go around our cross-country course," offered Mercedes.

"That is very kind. I'll take you up on that," said Mark, wishing that she had suggested that he come over and stay.

"It's so good for lovely Jessica and Felicia to have you here. I expect you'll set to and help them put this place to rights. They need a burly young man to do some of the heavy work," said Mercedes.

Mark looked at her sharply. There was no hint of facetiousness in her voice. She meant what she was saying. It looked like he was going to have to step out of character and think about doing good to others if he were to impress this aristocratic princess. If he hadn't been under the spell of an *idée fixe,* he might have wondered if he shouldn't have stuck with Diana, who was as heartless and selfish as himself.

Over the next week, Mark set to building partitions in the dining room. He had inspected all the available outbuildings, and the stables and Felicia had been correct. They were in such a state of disrepair that the only solution would be to bulldoze them and start again. He had never tried carpentry before, and he struggled with the set of rusty old tools that the Farthingtons possessed. The results of his efforts looked untidy, but the partitions worked, more or less.

Mark spent several hours a day simply mucking out. The area for each horse was much bigger than an ordinary loose box, and there was no drainage. By the time he had taken out the mucky straw, mopped the wet floor and set the place to rights, there was hardly time to exercise his horses. He didn't even get to Pevensy Park to practise over the jumps. He had ridden Patchwork. As far as he could tell, the comically patterned horse was nothing special. He had no desire to start riding it and suggested to Felicia and Jessica that for the time being, perhaps Serena should keep up the good work.

On one cold, wet, windy day, mounted on King, he came upon Ann, who was riding Dauntless across Neshbury Common.

"Oh! Hello!" she called. When she saw that it was Mark Lansdowne, she gasped in surprise. "I had no idea that you were in the area!" she exclaimed.

"I'm staying here for a while," said Mark in an agony of embarrassment.

"Are you staying with the Pevensys?" she asked.

"No. The Farthingtons," he muttered.

"The Farthingtons! I suppose your horses are stabled in the dining room," she chortled.

He glared at her.

"Wait until I tell Jill," she laughed.

Mark had cantered away, the sound of her mirth ringing in his ears. He wished he were dead. The thought of Jill Crewe finding out about his present situation was the absolute end. He almost packed up and left that evening, but he was determined to get to Tiddington and prove himself. If he won the open then perhaps Mercedes would fall in love with him. They could dispense with the big society wedding, run away to Gretna Green and he could move to Pevensy Park and have a happy ever after ending.

Chapter Fifteen – Tiddington Hunter Trials

Tiddington was several hours' drive from Chatton, so a lot of the competitors decided to go the day before and camp out.

"It'll be just like a jolly pony club camp," said Ann, who had never actually attended a pony club camp.

"But with grown-up drinking," said Henry.

"Yes, you're right, and I've got the most divine recipe for a champagne cocktail," said Ann.

"Hopefully, we'll take some more robust and nutritious provisions," said Henry. "I'm going to have to keep up my strength to compete against the famous Mark Lansdowne."

"Yes, Mummy will supply us with casseroles, and we can have a campfire to heat them with a tripod and a gipsy *pot au feu*," replied Ann, mixing her metaphors, her mind tripping away, dreaming up other gastronomic delights that might be served at an outdoor camping event.

She spent at least three hours on the phone chattering to other people about the arrangements. She was revelling in the latest news, which she imparted to everyone, that Mark Lansdowne was keeping his horses in the Miss Farthingtons' dining room. She had even considered contacting *Horse and Hound* with this juicy gossip but decided to wait until Jill came back to Chatton. Jill had already written several pieces for *Horse and Hound*, stretching her wings to include journalism as well as writing pony books. Such a story would be a coup. As Jill had several axes to grind with Malevolent Mark, it would also serve as revenge, the pen being mightier than the sword.

On Friday morning, the Chattonites who were going to Tiddington set off. Ann and Henry took Dauntless, Mark took British Brown and Kilkarny King, and also Patchwork, who he was riding in the novice as Serena was too busy at the riding school to go herself. James Bush took Jago, a big brown thoroughbred which he had ridden in the open event at Blossom Park. He was a wild and reckless horse. Like his owner, he lacked self-discipline and couldn't be relied on. In the past, James had not gotten him to peak fitness, but this time he had been working him hard since the end of November.

The Pevensys were out in force: Mercedes riding a young horse in the novice, Austin on Firefly, and Porsche taking both Mangala and Diablo to ride in the open. Susan was accompanying them. The three young women would sleep in the horsebox, and Austin had a little boy scout's tent.

Most of the competitors had arrived by mid-afternoon. They were stabling their horses overnight at a local riding school, which was walking distance from the camping ground. Quite a few riders had come from Norfolk. There was some friendly banter between competitors as they settled their horses in the loose boxes, filling water buckets and stuffing hay nets.

The weather was very cold, a wild wind roared across the fields, and the sun was obscured by grey louring clouds. The riders mounted and took their horses out for a walk along the lanes to work out any stiffness from the journey. Susan King rode Mangala for Porsche, and Ann found herself mounted on the magnificent British Brown who had competed at Burghley. She rode beside Henry on Dauntless, and Mark was ahead of them talking to Mercedes. The riders were eyeing up each other's mounts, calculating their chances in the competition. They got back to the stables and then set out in a group to walk the course, along with the helpers. Each of them was rugged up with heavy coats, snug hats, wellingtons and gloves.

The course was a big one, challenging, requiring both boldness and technical skill.

"I don't think that Porsche will get away with just driving her horses on relentlessly," Ann said quietly to Henry.

"Don't underestimate that young woman," he whispered, so they wouldn't be overheard. "I'm going to take it very carefully indeed. I'll aim to get around clear and not worry too much about speed."

"It will be interesting to see how the mighty Mark will manage," said Ann.

"James Bush is certainly going to have to lift his game, or he might just come to grief with a course like this," said Henry.

They got back to the camping grounds and the officials had built an enormous bonfire so everyone could gather around and socialise, rather than scurrying back to their respective camping beds. The orange and yellow flames leapt up towards the dark sky.

Ann handed out her champagne cocktail in paper cups.

"Hot toddies might have been more suitable than this," said Henry.

"This is delicious," said Susan, who was wearing a very pretty fur hat that framed her face.

Porsche gulped down a cupful, then helped herself to another.

Austin was drinking whisky from his hip flask with Porsche on one side and Susan on the other. They were a cosy little trio, and Ann's sharp eyes noticed the intimate touches between Susan and Austin. She would put her hand on his arm every now and again and gaze adoringly up into his eyes. He took it all in good part and played along with her.

"It's just the right balance of sweet and sour," said Mercedes, sipping delicately.

"Positively Bacchanalian! All we need now is some nymphs cavorting around the fire," said Austin, licking his lips lasciviously. Susan laughed too loud and too long at this witticism.

Mark and James were at Mercedes' side. Two virile young men, bristling at each other, determined to claim the girl. Mercedes seemed oblivious. If it wasn't horses, she wasn't interested. Mark obligingly talked about his horses. Then, he went on to gossip about other riders and their horses. Mercedes made the right noises, but she seemed preoccupied.

"Mummy and I are looking for another horse for me," she said. This was obviously what was on her mind. Mark changed tack and talked about the various horses that he knew were on the market. He wanted to sell British Brown, but he didn't even bother to mention this. Mercedes wanted a top competition prospect, not a horse that had competed and shown itself capable but without star quality.

"The trouble with trying to buy anything during an Olympic year is that the best horses are being jealously guarded," she commented.

"I've got a few horses you might be interested in," piped up James. "There's the Lancaster Bomber, who is showing a lot of promise."

"What are you riding tomorrow?" asked Mercedes politely. She'd seen the Lancaster Bomber at Blossom Park and Grassmere. He was a decent horse, but not what she was interested in.

"That's Jago. He's my best horse," replied James. Then, struck by inspiration, he said, "you know you could ride him tomorrow in the open and see what you think. I hadn't thought of selling him, but I suppose I might. If it were the right buyer."

"I remember you rode him at Blossom Park. He wasn't fit enough," replied Mercedes.

Mark laughed. This woman certainly knew her horses!

"Yes, there had been problems with his training schedule," said James huffily. "But now, he's as fit as a flea. He's a big strong horse. He's got a great jump in him, and he's fast."

"How is his dressage?" asked Mercedes, showing a glimmer of genuine interest.

"I don't go in for much flatwork," admitted James. "He probably needs a bit of training there."

"Can we go over and look at him?" asked Mercedes.

"Certainly," replied James.

Mark glowered as the two of them jumped in a Land Rover to drive the short distance to the stables. He would have offered to go with them, but somehow he couldn't bring himself to play second fiddle to such a nonentity as James Whatever-His-Name-Was.

The weather worsened on the following day. Sheets of rain fell in straight flat torrents. The stewards huddled together, discussing whether or not to cancel. The competitors and helpers were swathed in raincoats, with horse rugs draped over themselves like capes. They stared anxiously at the sky and walked around the squelchy ground feeling how soft it was. At nine o'clock, the skies cleared, and the rain ceased. The stewards ordered sawdust to be put down on the take-off and landing points of various jumps. The competitors screwed studs into the horses' hind hoofs.

The novice event was first on the schedule. Mercedes was riding one of the young ex-racehorses that she was retraining. Mark was on Patchwork. He rode beside her near the starting flags, waiting for the steward to call them. He wondered whether she was capable of any conversation that didn't involve horses. She was a cypher. Always cool, calm and collected and never betraying any strong emotion. He had to think of a plan to break through the unrippled surface of her personality. Perhaps there was nothing beneath her icy politeness. He decided that if he made no headway within a month, he would leave Oxfordshire and go somewhere else. He had no intention of staying at the Farthingtons any longer. He had some friends in the Midlands who might be able to put him up.

Several of the competitors had decided not to jump, packed up and driven off. They didn't want to risk their horses over such a tough course in these conditions. Mercedes decided that she would ride, but cautiously. There was no point in risking the legs of her novice horse, nor her own neck. She got around clear but with a very slow time. There were no other clear rounds. A lot of the horses had refused to jump the fence into a dark copse. The ground was sticky with mud, but what upset the horses was the sawdust that was scattered over the take-off point. They shied away from it, and there were slide marks everywhere in the mud.

Mark calculated that if he went clear and faster than Mercedes, then he would win. He would score brownie points by winning on Patchwork, not only with the Farthingtons but also hopefully with the Pevensys. He found Patchwork surprisingly good when pushed. He was brave and bold and responded to the lightest touch. Mark put it down to his superior riding technique rather than Serena's very thorough training on the flat. They got around clear and in a considerably faster time than Mercedes. Mark had won, and Mercedes was second.

The rain continued to hold off, and it was time for the open. The approach and landing of the higher jumps had had a few hours to dry a little with the strong wind. Mark and Mercedes were at a distinct advantage, having previously ridden the lower course. Mercedes was riding Jago around, accustoming herself to his way of going. It wasn't the first time she had ridden a horse in a competition without having ridden it previously. It was a mark of her competence that she could do this. She had courage, but she wasn't reckless.

Porsche also had courage, or perhaps it was merely a lack of imagination. She favoured her chances on Diablo, but she also had huge confidence in Mangala. Austin didn't care two hoots whether he did well or not. He just enjoyed the buzz of galloping and jumping. Henry was worried about Dauntless's legs and decided to withdraw at the last moment. Ann thoroughly approved of this decision. Mark was determined to win again, and he hoped that Kilkarny King might come first. British Brown second would be perfect. James had thought it a stroke of genius to offer Jago to Mercedes. If he managed to sell him, then he wanted to buy himself a very flashy little convertible. He would ask Mercedes out to dinner, and she would be sure to be impressed.

As Porsche was riding two horses, she went first on Mangala. His coat was still tinged with green, but she didn't care. She set off at a very fast gallop, over the first easy brush fence and then down the slope towards the drop fence into the quarry. He teetered on the edge, but she drove him on, making sure he didn't take a step back, which would constitute a refusal. He jumped down awkwardly and stumbled. The pain, which hadn't quite gone away since Blossom Park, streaked back through his foreleg. He cantered a few strides and faltered. Porsche wasn't having any of it, and flourishing her whip mercilessly, she sent him on. He galloped along the bottom of the quarry, but when it came to jumping out, up the slope and over a huge, solid four-feet jump, he hit the top rail and somersaulted. Porsche was thrown clear, but Mangala couldn't get up. The jump judges ran to grab his reins, but he wasn't going anywhere. They called over the loudspeaker for Henry to come and attend to him.

"He's in a very bad way," said Henry after examining the horse's legs. "I'm not sure that there'll be any coming back from this injury. I don't know whether we'll be able to get him up."

"Porsche has done it again. This is the second horse she's injured beyond recovery," whispered Ann, her face as white as chalk.

"Can't you give him a shot of something, we'll get him on his feet, and I'll lead him back," said Porsche, who had overheard Ann's remark and was looking thunderous. Her winged nostrils flared like a dragon about to breathe fire upon an enemy.

"You might want to call your own vet, a second opinion, but I'm not sure that he's going to make it," said Henry quietly.

"I've got to get Diablo warmed up," said Porsche. "I'll get Susan to go to the riding school and ring Mummy and tell her to organise it."

Mangala had fallen to one side of the jump, so with the help of several stewards, they were able to drag him away from the path of the next competitor. Ann ran back to the campsite to find some rugs to put over him. Henry managed to get the saddle off. Ann returned with a headcollar and two rugs. Gently they took off his bridle and put on the headcollar.

"Is he really going to have to be put down?" asked Susan, looking stricken.

"It's up to the Pevensy vet. I'm not making that call," said Henry gravely.

Mercedes had been told what had happened and ran up the hill. She threw herself upon Mangala's neck and wept. Memories of the loss of her beloved Banjo flooded her. Porsche had staked him on the wing of a jump, and he had had to be put down. No one watching her would think that she was incapable of strong emotion. If James or Mark had been present, they might have taken advantage of her distress to wrap their arms around her, but the role of comforter fell to Ann.

"Come on, my dear," she said soothingly. "Henry will stay with him until your own vet arrives. Don't you have to ride Jago, or are you going to withdraw?"

"No, you're right," said Mercedes, lifting her head and dashing the tears from her eyes. "One must never give up. Never give in to an excess of sentimentality. Just keep that Porsche away from me!"

Mark was the next competitor on British Brown. He wanted to get the hang of the course before he rode Kilkarny King. He had heard what had happened as the news passed from person to person around the course. He had seen Mercedes haring up the field and had been tempted to run after her, but he held back. There was nothing he could do, and he was due to ride as soon as the course was clear.

The steward counted him down, and he set off. He had years of experience riding around the hardest courses in Britain. He knew that he was a better rider than any of them here and Brownie and he had been partners for three years. He rode at each jump with every ounce of judgment that he possessed. His horse rose to the occasion, and he got around clear in quite a reasonable time. Dismounting, he led Brownie back to the horse truck. He wasn't used to having to act as a groom as well as a rider. He threw a light rug over him and led him up the ramp into the horsebox to keep him out of the wind. Then, he led King down and tacked up. He would ride around until the stewards called him for his next round.

After Mangala's fall, more of the riders had withdrawn, and there wasn't that long to wait. Austin was trotting around, waiting to be called. He set off, cantered steadily through the start and popped over the brush, then to the lip of the quarry, where he disappeared from view. Two other riders set off, and they too disappeared into the quarry. There were no announcements of falls over the loudspeaker.

Then, Mercedes on Jago was called. Her face was white, but she was composed and, as usual riding in a perfect position. The big brown thoroughbred looked different. With James, he had always been ragged and wild, but with Mercedes in the saddle, he was held well together. His neck was slightly bent, his eyes looking forward attentively, and his legs moving rhythmically beneath him. They set off, and Mark watched admiringly. If nothing else, this woman could ride to perfection. He didn't care if she was better than him. It would be a constant challenge to match her. Together they would conquer the heights of international three-day eventing. He decided that the time had come to make a move.

Austin rode back through the finish.

"How did you go?" asked a young woman standing near the finishing line.

"I had two stops," he shouted back cheerfully.

Then the two other riders and horses came in. Mark was called on King before Mercedes finished the course. He imagined that she was out there somewhere, and he had to ride like a hero to catch her up. Of course, this wasn't practical, but he was feeling unusually romantic. His feelings for Mercedes were having a very strange effect on him.

Kilkarny King wasn't happy. Perhaps it was living in a dining room or the muddy going. He just wasn't right. Mark pushed him on vigorously, riding with determination, but the big, grey gelding was hesitant, shaking his head, and then most unusually, he ran out at the water jump. It was all Mark could do to get him into the cold lake water at a second attempt. They splashed through and jumped out, and King was in a very bad mood. With one stop they had no chance of winning.

Mercedes had got round clear on Jago, and he had impressed her hugely. She put aside her feelings about Mangala and asked James how much he wanted for him. She knew that because her family were wealthy, people often tried to take advantage, and certainly James did ask for a substantial sum. She bargained with him, and they settled on what she thought was reasonable for a strong, fit horse that needed a great deal of dressage training to do well in three-day eventing. James would have to shop around for a second-hand convertible.

Porsche was called last, and she got some cold looks from people who thought her both careless and heartless. She paid no attention. She rode in her usual style, but Diablo baulked at the lip of the quarry, and she slid over his head and tumbled down the steep side. A few people laughed, and one even cheered. No one thought much of her after what had happened to Mangala.

Within half an hour, the winners were announced. Mark was fourth on Kilkarny King, a tall girl on a black horse was third, Mark was second on British Brown, and Mercedes was first on Jago.

"Well done," said Mark, warmly shaking her hand. "Might I take you out to dinner tomorrow night to celebrate your success," he said politely.

"Oh!" said Mercedes, somewhat startled. Young men didn't usually ask her out on dates. "Well, yes, that would be very pleasant," she replied politely.

Mangala had been put down, and his body hauled away by a farmer with a tractor. It had cast a pall on the atmosphere. The clouds cleared by late afternoon, and thin winter sunlight shone over the wet fields. Everyone packed up and drove home.

Chapter Sixteen – The Blue Jackdaw

Mark was thinking about where to take Mercedes for dinner. Not that many restaurants would be open on Sunday night. He would have to ask a local for recommendations. In the end, he rang Ann. She wasn't his favourite person, and he knew she was a bit of a gossip but full of good ideas.

"Hello, Ann, this is Mark Lansdowne," he said.

Ann was shocked. Mark Lansdowne ringing her at eleven o'clock on a Sunday morning was certainly not a regular occurrence. Mark ringing her at all was unusual. She had thought that he lumped her in with Jill as an undesirable.

"Good morning," said Ann, gathering her wits. "What can I do for you?"

"I am taking Mercedes Pevensy out to dinner tonight, and I wondered if you could recommend a good restaurant that might be open on Sunday night?"

"Golly gosh!" gasped Ann, amazed that such a delicious piece of news had dropped into her lap.

"People do go out to dinner, you know," snapped Mark, thinking he had made a mistake in ringing Ann.

"I'll tell you what; there is a charming little *trattoria* in Oxford that serves delicious pasta and the most divine tiramisu for dessert. Did you know that 'tiramisu' means 'pull you to me' in Italian?"

"No, I didn't know that," said Mark, thinking that a cheap little Italian restaurant hadn't exactly been his plan.

"After dinner, you could take her to The Blue Jackdaw in Crosby Street. It's a jazz club that is all the rage. It will make you look like a cool cat."

"Really?" exclaimed Mark, thinking that the last thing he imagined himself as was a cool cat.

"What about transport?" asked Ann. "You've only got your enormous horsebox, haven't you?"

"I thought a taxi," said Mark shortly. Ann was an exceedingly annoying know-it-all, but he had to admit that she was bright.

"You can borrow my little run around if you like?" said Ann.

"That is very kind of you. I'll walk around and pick it up this evening," said Mark hanging up before he screamed in anguish.

Henry and Ann sat down to a cosy Sunday supper of cheese rarebit, one of Henry's favourites. He stretched out comfortably in front of the fire.

"I guess I should make tracks and get back to my place. Yesterday's events have tired me out, and I've got an early morning appointment at Richardson's dairy farm tomorrow morning," he said.

"I've got a much better idea," said Ann. "I want you to take me to The Blue Jackdaw. I promise you it will be vastly entertaining."

"That sounds mysterious," said Henry, going along with whatever Ann suggested.

Ann leapt up the stairs to get changed.

"Is what I'm wearing alright?" asked Henry sleepily.

"No one is going to look at you, I promise," said Ann. "But I do want to look the part."

After ten minutes, she descended the cottage stairs, and Henry opened his eyes. She was wearing a very short, pale blue shift dress with high heels. A jazzy type of necklace was looped around her neck, and she had a tiny pale blue clutch purse that perfectly matched her dress.

"You look rather …." Henry couldn't quite find the right words.

"Chic?" suggested Ann, cocking her head at him cheekily.

"Chic," he confirmed, but doubtfully. He was beginning to think that he would have to marry Ann and tie her pregnant to the kitchen sink, or she might become far too fashionable and modern for a boring country vet.

Henry and Ann often went to The Blue Jackdaw, and the man at the door greeted them in a friendly manner and took their coats. After the crisp, cold air outside, it was a relief to be enveloped in a smoky fug.

There was a singer on the raised dais at the end of the room. Her husky voice was rasping but, at the same time, melodious, a whiskey and cigarette voice. She was what would be called a 'comfortable armful'. Her hair was carefully styled, short and curled upwards at the ends with a velvet headband holding it in place. Her dress was of the same velvet, rich red, and plush, with a low neckline. She wore a choker that dazzled with paste diamonds, matching her chunky earrings. Her eyebrows were shaped like half-moons, thick and arched over eyes that were made up with smoky grey eyeshadow. Her nose was rather broad, but with small nostrils, her cheeks round and rosy like apples and her luscious lips were painted bright red, accentuating her best feature, her perfect white teeth. She was strumming a ukulele.

Behind her was a theatrical backdrop, a crescent moon filled with red silk flowers and striped curtains of dark purple and dull gold. There was a suited man playing the saxophone on stage beside her and another man seated behind with an acoustic guitar. A dozen couples slunk around the floor in front of her, their arms entwined around each other's bodies, in tune with the beguiling music.

Two cigarette girls dressed up in French burlesque style were circulating around the small tables where the customers were sitting. Ann waved a cheery greeting to other people, including a table of four older men who looked like they were on the run from the London underworld.

"I don't believe it!" exclaimed Henry. "Look! There's Mark Lansdowne and Mercedes Pevensy over there, sitting at the table near the stage. Who would have thought that those two would come to such a place?"

"It was my suggestion," said Ann smugly. "I told you tonight would be vastly entertaining. Do you think Mark will succeed in his determined courtship?"

"I have no idea," said Henry. "I hope you're not thinking that we should go and interrupt them."

"Not at all. I'm waiting for you to slide me into your arms and onto the dance floor," said Ann laughing at him. "From there I should have a good vantage point to keep an eye on them."

Chapter Seventeen – A New Show Pony

A week after the Tiddington event, early on Sunday morning, Lavender went out to the stable yard to feed Black Boy and Rapide. Her mother had told her that there was no need to go to church, and a long ride with Ruby was planned. They were going to take a picnic lunch. She was startled when a truck trundled into the stable yard, and her mother popped out from around the corner.

"What's happening?" asked Lavender, looking confused.

A man jumped down from the cab, went round the back and lowered the ramp.

The most beautiful pony danced down and stood in the yard looking around with wide-open brown eyes fringed with impossibly long eyelashes.

"Lavender, darling, this is Summer Fancy!" crowed her mother. "The most fantastic show pony for you that we've bought from Thea!"

Lavender stood rooted to the spot. She felt like her hair was sticking out from her head. Her mind was whirling like a Catherine wheel. She couldn't utter a word.

"You bought him off Thea," she echoed.

"Yes, apparently Thea wanted to do gymkhana games rather than showing," said Mrs E-H.

"I know, she didn't want to do showing," said Lavender. "Are they going to buy her a pony for doing games?"

"Yes, I believe they are," said her mother. "It was the chance of a lifetime to buy this pony. He is going to make it to the top."

"Wow!" said Lavender. "He is beautiful, but I'm not sure about him. He's so special that Thea's mother would never let her jump him or do anything but walk, trot and canter on the flat. She didn't even want her to take him out hacking."

"That seems rather extreme, but then again, he was tremendously expensive," replied Mrs E-H.

At this point, Ruby arrived in the stable yard.

"Thea's pony!" she exclaimed. "Has she come to visit? Are we all going for a ride?"

"Not exactly," said Lavender slowly. "It seems Mummy and Daddy have bought Summer Fancy for me."

"Wow! You lucky duck!" said Ruby, but not in a jealous way. "He sure be the prettiest pony I've ever seen. That tiny white star, dead centre in his forehead, an' he got a perfick 'ead."

"He is beautiful," agreed Lavender.

"So, 'e's definitely got one of the stables, which of them others is gonna be stuck in the field?" asked Ruby.

Mrs E-H looked down at the ground and shuffled her feet.

"Mummy, we've only got two loose boxes. Are we going to get another one built? Or is Rapide going back to the Pevensys?" asked Lavender.

"No, I've talked to Aggie, and the present arrangement that Rapide stay here during term time will remain the same. I'm afraid we're going to have to sell Black Boy."

"Sell ol' Black Boy!" exclaimed Ruby in horror.

"You've grown so much. He's too small for you now," said Mrs E-H adopting an imminently reasonable voice.

"You can't sell him!" shouted Lavender, her brain racing like an engine. "No! No! I don't care about Summer Fancy. I want to keep Black Boy. I love him. He's still my best friend."

"Lavender, we've let you have a dog. Now, you've got this gorgeous pony who will take you to the top, and you can ride the Pevensys' showjumper. You are being very selfish!" said her mother impatiently. "Porsche Pevensy has found a buyer. A family called the Bullhorns."

"I don't care about winning at shows. I only want Black Boy. He is my heart pony! I love him!" pleaded Lavender and broke down into heart-rending sobs.

"You're being ridiculous," snapped her mother, who was annoyed that this amazing purchase was not appreciated by her selfish daughter who didn't seem to understand the importance of winning. "Susan is coming around soon to see him. She played a big part in us being able to buy him, her and Porsche. Hopefully, she can talk some sense into you, you ungrateful little monster!"

"I don't want to talk to her. She's in cahoots with the hateful Porsche who has done this to hurt me!" cried Lavender as she turned around and fled inside to lie on her bed and sob.

Ruby stood there with her mouth open.

"Do you want me to do something with him? We still have to muck out the loose boxes. Perhaps he should go in the field?" asked Ruby taking a practical approach.

"I'm not sure about him going in the field. He might hurt himself," said Mrs E-H helplessly. She was at a loss regarding Lavender's reaction.

Ruby was devastated at the news that Black Boy was to be sold, but she didn't collapse in a weeping heap. That wasn't her way. She kept busy, putting Black Boy and Rapide out in the field. It looked like the planned ride wasn't going to happen. She tied Summer Fancy to a ring in the wall and set to cleaning the loose boxes. She emptied one entirely, wheelbarrowing out loads of straw. Then she swilled around a small amount of hot water and disinfectant. She had read somewhere that a new pony or horse in the stable yard meant a complete clean of the loose box.

While she was waiting for the floor to dry, she stripped off Fancy's rugs and brushed him down. She was wondering whether it might be alright to try him. He was certainly stunning, and she longed to find out what it was like to ride such a pony. Thea had described him as a clockwork mouse.

Ruby hung around and hung around. The floor dried, and she piled in an extra thick bed of straw, banking up the edges to exclude any errant draughts and stop Fancy from getting stuck when he lay down. She untied him from the ring in the wall and led him into the loose box. He didn't seem to appreciate her efforts. He whirled around in circles, rushing towards the half-door and gazing out and then turning this way and that as if he were looking for an escape. He wasn't settling. He didn't seem to like his new surroundings. Ruby decided that she should go and fetch Rapide and put him in the next-door loose box so that Fancy had some company. Rapide didn't like being brought in when it was meant to be his time, either for riding or for hanging out in the field. He looked sullen and unhappy and let his tongue hang out of the corner of his mouth. Fancy didn't seem any more settled and was walking in circles in the box and pushing his chest against the lower door. Ruby decided she would shut the top door in case he tried to jump out.

It was lunchtime, and she was hungry. There had been no food at home for breakfast, and she had counted on Lavender supplying the sandwiches for lunch. Finally, she was so hungry by one o'clock that she went up to the house and knocked tentatively on the kitchen door. No-one answered. She turned the handle. It wasn't locked. Slipping off her boots as Mrs E-H was very fussy about clean floors, she crept into the kitchen. There were the remnants of a pork pie on the kitchen table, and it took every ounce of Ruby's willpower not to snaffle it up. She slid across the floor and out into the passageway.

"'Ullo, is anyone 'ere?" she said in a low voice.

There was silence. She went up the stairs to Lavender's room. The door was shut.

"Lavender, are you in there?" she whispered. No answer. She opened the door, and there was Lavender lying on the bed face down, with her boots on the counterpane which was utterly *verboten* in this house.

"Lavender is me. Are you orright?" asked Ruby.

"What do you think, of course, I'm not. This is what I was afraid of all along, and now Black Boy is going to be sold, and I'm not going to be able to bear to even look at Summer Fancy as if it is his fault, but it's not really his fault at all. How am I going to bear this?" she asked plaintively.

"Perhaps if we go downstairs, 'av sumfin ta eat we can make a plan," said Ruby, thinking of the pork pie. "I don't fink your mother is around. It's pretty quiet."

"I'm never going to eat again," cried Lavender melodramatically.

"Well, I've dun all the work this mornin', and I'm kinda 'ungry," said Ruby. "I gotta eat!"

"I'm sorry," sniffled Lavender. "Let's go downstairs, and you can eat."

"Summer Fancy is pretty unsettled. I've shut the top stable door, so he doan try an' jump out," said Ruby.

"Why don't we take Rapide and Black Boy for a ride. We could just ride and ride and never come back," said Lavender in a rush of desperation.

"We have to take some food, and blankets, and horse nuts," said Ruby, trying to be practical. "We might want to take all three ponies, and one of them can carry some supplies."

"No, no, no!" declared Lavender. "The whole point is not to take Summer Fancy, and maybe he can go back to Thea, or Mummy can sell him and not Black Boy."

"But Thea doan want 'im. Think of 'is feelin's," said Ruby, suddenly seeing a way through this mess. I'm gonna saddle up Black Boy and Rapide, and mebbe we can come up wiv a plan while we ride."

Lavender stood there helplessly. She was wilting like a broken flower. Ruby went to the field, and Black Boy was standing near the gate looking downcast.

"You poor boy," she said softly, slipping on his headcollar.

Lavender was drooping in the stable yard and couldn't do more than sob into Black Boy's mane.

Ruby had to do all the tacking up.

"Come on," she said impatiently, wondering if she were going to have to hoist Lavender into the saddle.

Eventually, they were both mounted and riding out onto the road.

"Let's go over to Neshbury Common," said Ruby, thinking that a familiar ride might help Lavender get to grips with what was happening. She glanced over at her friend, hoping that riding might work its magic. Lavender was humming an airy-fairy tuneless nonsensical rhyme. She was acting a bit loony.

Ruby had been so busy that she hadn't had time to process the significance of what had happened. It was her that was going to be affected most by this change of circumstances. She would lose the pony that she rode and competed on. Lavender now not only had the use of Rapide, the showjumper, but also a fantabulous new show pony.

They walked on towards the woods, and Ruby began to concentrate on the prospect of her future. She would be reinstated as the poorly paid groom, and perhaps she would be allowed to exercise Rapide and Fancy, but it was unlikely that she would be riding in any pony club rallies or gymkhanas. And, it wasn't just that she would lose her chance to compete. She had grown to love Black Boy as if he were her own. In some ways, she felt that she belonged to him. Now it seemed that he would be lost forever. She had no idea what the Bullhorn family was like, but if it was organised by Porsche, then they were sure to be horrors, part of Porsche's dark plot of revenge against Lavender and herself.

They came to the woods, and it was gloomy under the trees. Ruby's mind was clouded with dark thoughts. She could see no way through it all. Lavender's idea of riding away with Black Boy and Rapide wasn't practical. It wasn't like being pioneers in America, where they could 'go west' and make new lives for themselves on the gold fields or build a farm on the prairie. England was a densely populated country, and there would be little chance of finding a refuge where they could hide and survive.

Ruby's mind began to buzz. She had to think of a solution. If Black Boy was sold, it would be as if she were losing part of her soul. Lavender was as limp as a wet rag and didn't seem capable of thinking of anything. She would give in and get carried along with events. If something was to be done, it would be up to herself, decided Ruby.

They got back to the stables. Fancy whinnied wildly when he heard the ponies clip-clopping into the stable yard.

"He's been in all day. He needs to be ridden, or at least put out in the field for a while," said Ruby, being practical.

"I don't want to ride him. It will be like giving in," said Lavender sullenly.

Ruby would have loved to have a ride, and she didn't see that it would make much difference one way or another. Mrs E-H wasn't going to give in. Inevitably, they would keep Summer Fancy, and Black Boy would be sold. She led the show pony out to the field and let him loose.

"I doan suppose we could take Black Boy to the Miss Farvingtons," she said idly. "P'haps they could hide 'im for us, so he doan go to them Bullhorns."

"I don't think they would agree to that," said Lavender dolefully.

"Ya remember in them Jill books, there woz that girl Dinah, who stole the ponies and lived in the forest," said Ruby thoughtfully.

"It's winter. How could we live in a forest in the middle of winter?" asked Lavender helplessly.

Ruby saw then that Lavender was not going to do anything. She would be carried along on the tide of events that had been orchestrated by the dastardly Porsche. If anyone was going to have to save Black Boy then it would be herself.

Chapter Eighteen – The Stolen Pony

Jill travelled down from Scotland and was staying in Chatton for a week before she went to London to board the plane for Australia. She had been invited to stay with the Heywards and go on a showjumping tour down the east coast.

Early on Monday morning, she walked up the driveway to Pool Cottage and let herself in with a key. She loved that moment of stepping over the threshold into her very own domain. Pool Cottage had been signed over to her when her mother had married Richard. Of course, Ann had put her stamp upon the place, but Jill didn't mind that at all. She adopted the same attitude as the faithful Henry when it came to Ann's new hobby of collecting *objets d'art.* Ann would scour second-hand and antique shops for unusual and interesting bric-a-brac, and now the tiny cottage was decorated with brightly coloured blankets and misshapen ornaments that Ann had discovered and carried home with pride.

Jill went into the kitchen to make herself a cup of tea. There were the remnants of a rather delicious-looking date and walnut loaf in a tin in the food cupboard. She spread two slices with thick golden butter and sat down to enjoy her repast. Travelling on a train always gave her an enormous appetite.

The phone rang, and she answered.

"Hello."

"Who's this?" came a sharp female voice.

"It's Jill Crewe," she replied.

"Jill! What on earth are you doing there?" retorted a voice she now recognised. Susan King.

"Pool Cottage is my home," she replied, wondering what on earth was wrong. Susan sounded fraught. "Can I help you with anything? Or perhaps leave a message for Ann? She's not home."

"Oh, Jill! Something awful has occurred. Black Boy has been stolen!" Jill detected a false note in Susan's voice. Perhaps Susan didn't think this was 'awful' at all.

"Stolen?"

"Yes. Am I speaking English? Stolen. He has been taken from his field in the night, and just before the Bullhorns were coming to see him to buy him."

"Buy him?" echoed Jill.

"Do you have to repeat everything I say?"

"Who are the Bullhorns when they're at home?"

"Really, Jill! You act as if you should know who everyone is. You're no longer the Chatton Princess!"

"I never was a Chatton Princess," snapped Jill. "I think that is a perfectly reasonable question. Anyway, why was Black Boy being sold? Lavender loves him. She would never sell him."

"Lavender is a child. It's not up to her," said Susan smugly. "Porsche Pevensy and I managed to pull off such a coup, and dear Evelyn bought the most fantastic show pony, Summer Fancy for Lavender. Anyway, she's shot up like a bean pole, and let's face it, Black Boy is just about a beginner's pony and not much else."

Jill felt anger broiling deep within her outraged breast. Now, the truth was coming out. Porsche and Susan in cahoots was a poisonous combination. Poor Lavender must be utterly distraught. Since Jill had first met her, the young girl had been afraid of her mother's show pony ambitions. The Bullhorns sounded ghastly. Just their name said it all.

"I must go and see Lavender!" said Jill. "Goodbye."

She hung up the receiver. She was assailed with a memory. Dinah Dean who had stolen three horses that were going to be slaughtered. She had taken them deep into the forest and slept in the roots of a tree. Jill had found her and taken her food. This felt like history repeating itself. But Black Boy! Her darling first pony. If he were to be sold, then she would buy him even if she had to sell Sky Diver, her dressage horse, to pay for him!

Jill was so disturbed that she left half a slice of date and walnut loaf on her plate and ran out of the cottage and all the way down the road to the Ellison-Heath's house. Evelyn was shrieking in outrage. Lavender was weeping, and Ruby was comforting her.

There were two village bobbies, one writing in his notebook, the other walking around the field looking for clues. Mr Ellison-Heath, who was usually lurking in the shadows, was there in force speaking to the policeman and announcing that he was going to contact the insurance company.

"So, this here pony, he was insured?" said the bobby, with a sharp meaningful look.

"Yes, of course, he was insured. All of our property is insured," retorted Mr E-H.

"He was valuable, was he?"

"Well, not particularly. The other one, Summer Fancy, he cost us a fortune," replied Mr E-H proudly, as if spending a lot of money on a pony was something to boast about.

"That's what I don't understand," shrilled Mrs E-H. "Why take Black Boy when Rapide and Summer Fancy are much more valuable?"

The bobby raised his head to look at her sharply.

"Why were you selling this Black . . ." he looked down at his notebook to remember, "Boy? Was there something wrong with him?"

"No, of course not," said Mr E-H impatiently. "We bought the new pony, and we had to sell one of the others. The brown one, he belongs to the Pevensys."

At this point, the policeman looked mystified.

"Why have you got one of the Pevensys' ponies here? Do they know you've got him?"

"Of course, they know!" shrieked Mrs E-H. "Do you think we've stolen him?"

The policeman shot her a dark, suspicious look. This case was getting more complicated by the minute.

"They took Black Boy because he was in the field. The other two were in stables," volunteered Ruby.

"Surely, it be easier to take a pony out of a loose box than run around a field catching him," said the policeman, exercising his logical faculties.

"It would be quieter leading him through a gate than clattering across the stable yard," said Ruby.

"Who are you?" asked the policeman.

"I'm the groom. I muck out the boxes and exercise them," said Ruby defensively.

Lavender was looking wan and washed out with dark shadows under her eyes. She was crushed and confused.

"A cuppa tea would go down well," said the other policeman who walked over from his investigations in the field.

"Really!" shrieked Mrs E-H. "I demand that the police chief come and look into this. You two don't seem to be getting anywhere."

Obviously, she was unaware that cups of tea fuelled and lubricated all members of police forces everywhere.

Jill's mind was racing. She decided there was no point in leaping in and demanding explanations. They were going to sell Black Boy. The buyers had been coming today, and during the night, he had disappeared. To her, it was obvious, Ruby and Lavender had cooked up this plot between them. The timing was too coincidental for it to have been a random theft. Although, Lavender did look genuinely distraught. Perhaps Ruby had acted alone. Jill pondered the best way to tackle Ruby. She would shake her until she got the truth out of her. One way or the other, she would get her to tell where she had taken him. Then she would make her move and demand that he be sold to her, not to the undoubtedly ghastly Bullhorns. He would go to Scotland, and live there until the day he died, which hopefully was a long time in the distant future.

"Did you find any clues?" Mr E-H demanded, turning on the policeman who had been walking around the field.

"We're continuing with our investigation," said the other one with dignity.

"It's Monday. Lavender should be at school. I've got a committee meeting this morning and then a lunch. My husband should be at work. We can't stand around here all day while you two muddle around," said Mrs E-H.

"But what about the others? Perhaps someone will come and take them if no one is 'ere?" said Ruby. "I doan need ta go to school. I'll stay 'ere and guard them."

It struck Jill that this was putting the fox in charge of the henhouse. No one else seemed to suspect Ruby.

"I'll stay here with you," said Jill, thinking it was an ideal time to get the truth out of her.

"Evelyn, you need to go to the hardware shop and buy some very strong padlocks that we can put on the stable doors. Perhaps a chain and padlock for the field gate," said Mr E-H. "Have you finished now?" he asked the policemen peremptorily.

"We'll be looking into this," said one of the policemen meaningfully. He wasn't satisfied with the answers he had received.

"You do that," said Mr E-H and turned on his heel and stalked to the house.

Mrs E-H went upstairs to change into her committee outfit. Lavender put on her school uniform, and they all left. Ruby and Jill eyed each other across the kitchen table.

"Where did you take him?" demanded Jill, cutting straight to the chase.

"Wot?" replied Ruby, feigning confusion over the meaning of the question.

"Where did you take Black Boy?" repeated Jill, enunciating each word very clearly.

"I doan know wot yore talking 'bout," replied Ruby, her little eyes glinting.

Jill realised that Ruby wasn't going to be the easiest nut to crack.

"It's obvious. You took him so he wouldn't be sold to the Bullhorns. I don't want him sold to the Bullhorns either. I want him back, and I'll take him to Scotland where he'll be safe."

Ruby looked mutinous.

"I didna take 'im," she declared. "Ya can't prove I did!"

Jill realised that she was going to get nowhere with this. She would have to try a different tack.

"I've got to go back to Pool Cottage. Don't think you're going to get away with this. I want my pony back," said Jill and stalked out and down the driveway. Perhaps she had done the wrong thing, alerting Ruby to her suspicions. She would have to try a different way.

She returned to the cottage deep in thought. Where would Ruby have taken him? Perhaps she had a relative where he might be hidden. She didn't even know where Ruby lived. She needed to talk to Ann.

When she got back to the cottage, she rang Henry.

"Have you heard?" she said, trying to suppress a hysterical note in her voice. "Black Boy has been stolen. I need to talk to Ann."

"Why?" asked Henry in an exaggeratedly reasonable voice. "Do you think she knows something about it?"

"No, of course not," snapped Jill. "But where is she? I got here early this morning, and she was gone. Black Comedy and Totty are in the field."

"She was meeting up with some of her college buddies, and they were having a revision breakfast," said Henry.

"A revision breakfast?" queried Jill, "a revised breakfast?" She had never heard of such a thing.

"It was Ann's idea," he replied. "She's only got a half-day today, should be back by lunchtime."

"Thanks," said Jill and hung up. Her brain didn't seem to be working. She decided to ride back to the Ellison-Heaths' and keep an eye on what Ruby was up to.

She tacked up and mounted Black Comedy. She would ride up behind the Ellison-Heath property. There was a path that led above the hill and she remembered a copse, where she could stand and watch unobserved. As Ruby had only taken Black Boy the night before, it was unlikely that she would go to him this morning. She would be cautious, waiting for the hoo-ha to die down.

Jill made her way to the high ground that looked down on the Ellison-Heaths' property. Ruby was riding in the field on Summer Fancy.

"The cheeky little girl," said Jill to Black Comedy. "I wonder if she has permission to ride that pony."

Ruby and Summer Fancy were trotting circles.

"He's certainly a very pretty pony," muttered Jill. "And Ruby is not a bad rider."

After trotting for ten minutes, they cantered. Summer Fancy did seem perfectly trained. He held himself together and cantered with a steady, even beat. Eventually, Ruby walked to cool him down, and she led him back to the stable yard, where she untacked and rubbed him all over. Jill could not fault her. She rode correctly. She cooled down and attended to the pony in a copybook manner.

Jill was hungry. She hadn't planned to spend her time in Chatton loitering around and spying on a small girl. She had wanted to visit her old friends, going back to her roots and trying to regain her sense of self that had recently been fractured. She decided to ride back to see Ann. Together they would make a plan. Never had she felt such a need for her best friend's company.

Ann was thrilled to see Jill. But, her joy at reuniting with her soon dissipated upon hearing the news that Black Boy was to be sold and now he had been stolen.

"I think you're right about Ruby. It's definitely the sort of enterprising thing that she might do. You know that she dyed Porsche's horse bright green the night before the hunter trials. It was a hoot, but unfortunately, it's set off this train of events. I do get on well with her, but I don't know that she'll confide in me. She would probably think that we would try and rescue the pony. I just can't imagine what the long-term plan is. They can't keep him hidden forever unless they sneak him out of the county, and then she still wouldn't be able to ride him. Perhaps she acted on the spur of the moment and didn't really think it through."

"What about Lavender?" asked Jill. "Do you think she was in on it?"

"I don't know. Somehow, I doubt it. Lavender is raher timid when it comes to rebelling against social convention."

"Unlike Ruby," said Jill grimly. "I've got to buy Black Boy back. Do you think I can persuade the Ellison-Heaths? That is assuming we can find him."

"I think that money talks with them," said Ann. "If you offer enough money, they'll sell to the highest bidder."

"That's another issue. I don't have any money," groaned Jill.

"But you seem very comfortable now. You know, living at the castle, owning this cottage and now you're swanning off for an extended holiday in Australia," said Ann, puzzled.

"That's a whole other story," said Jill. "I haven't had time to get you up to speed. All Richard's trust fund, and the Lansdownes' have been stolen by the lawyer. We're now penniless. We're trying to set up the stables as a going concern. Linda and Hugh, you do know they've just got married, and John, who worked in the stables are my business partners. We have an equal quarter each, and we're trying to make a go of it."

"How admirably socialistic! But you're going to Australia?" queried Ann.

"Well, Mummy said that I must go. It was such a splendid opportunity. I've got to take some advertising material, and I'm supposed to be spreading the word through the Antipodes, so that rich Australians come to the Scottish Highlands for a riding holiday."

"Gosh!" exclaimed Ann. "You're certainly thinking big! It does sound a long way to go on a riding holiday?"

"The Heywards are paying my fare and all the expenses, and there's . . ." Jill tailed off.

Ann wrinkled up her forehead.

"That suddenly makes sense!" she declared. "Mark Lansdowne has turned up in Chatton, and he is staying with the Farthingtons. They're two funny old ladies, and he's keeping two of his competition horses in the dining room."

"What? The dining room? That's not possible!" cried Jill.

"I know it is so amusing. I was thinking of writing in to *Horse and Hound* to tell them but thought you might want to do a whole article."

"I can't think about that now," said Jill. "It's Black Boy who is important. What on earth has that dratted girl done with him?"

"We could try and get it out of her," said Ann. "But she's a determined little thing. I imagine she can keep her trap shut."

"Do you know where she lives?" asked Jill.

"Henry gave her a lift home once. It's a dreadful dreary little place called Ditching Hollow. She lives in a tumbledown caravan with a sick mother and a largely absent father. I can't imagine that she's hidden Black Boy there. It would be too obvious. She must have taken him far enough away so that he wouldn't be recognised by any locals."

"Do you think we could drive by her house and check it out," said Jill, "just in case."

"We could drive past, I guess," said Ann. "You know if it was Ruby, I think she's done it for the best of reasons. She really is a decent girl."

Jill growled. She was seeing everything through a glass darkly.

They set out in Ann's little car.

"Why is Mark Lansdowne in Chatton, anyway?" asked Jill.

"He's in pursuit of Mercedes Pevensy. Honestly, it was like watching a movie at the Christmas party. He arrived with Diana Barton-Tompkin and was just struck down with love at the sight of Mercedes. Poor Diana flounced off, and Mark has come down here to court her."

"What's this Mercedes like?" asked Jill idly.

"I don't know her very well. She's extremely reserved. Polite. Cool. Detached. But she's a great rider, very correct and thinks a lot of her horses. They say she's wildly ambitious. There was a hunter trials at Tiddington, and the three Pevensys went, and Susan with them. Austin came nowhere as usual, but he doesn't care. Porsche rode one of her geldings to death, and he had to be put down, and Diablo, you know that horrible black horse that Susan owned, tipped her head first down the side of the quarry. One person actually cheered as she tumbled down. But Mercedes won it! Riding James Bush's big gelding, Jago. She's bought it now, and James is whizzing around town in a second-hand convertible. He had his eye on Mercedes too, but he's not in the same league."

"Everyone is moving on," said Jill. She liked to think that things in Chatton stayed the same. That she could always come back and pick up her life if she wanted to. Nothing was the same anymore.

Chapter Nineteen – Jill the Super Sleuth

Jill and Ann drove past Ruby's caravan at Ditching Hollow that afternoon. Jill had never imagined that such a dismal area existed near the idyllic village of Chatton. Hidden down a small twisting road littered with potholes it was a clutch of broken-down huts and caravans set on a desolate stretch of land. Mongrel dogs lay in the dirt and barked as they drove by. There was nowhere to hide a pony. Black Boy was not there.

On the following day, Jill decided that Ruby might set out to check on Black Boy, wherever she had hidden him. She rode back to the copse, taking a supply of drinks and sandwiches in an old saddle bag that she had found in the tack room.

She arrived at the copse very early. She saw the Ellison-Heath parents and Lavender get in the car. Presumably, Lavender was off to school, and Mr E-H was going to the station to catch a train to work. Ruby was there, mucking out. She had both Rapide and Summer Fancy tied up in the yard, and she stripped off their rugs and groomed them.

Jill was impatient. She hated all this hanging around. The work of a private detective was not as exciting and glamorous as it sounded. Finally, Ruby put Summer Fancy in the field, carefully chaining and padlocking the gate and then saddled Rapide.

"Now, my girl, take me to my pony," said Jill, willing Ruby to decide to ride to where she had hidden Black Boy.

"This looks promising," said Jill to Black Comedy. Ruby was trotting down the grass verge to the end of the road. She had an air of purpose as she rode. Hopefully, this was no ambling ride around the lanes. She also had a knapsack on her back which bulged. As if it might be filled with horse nuts or some other mysterious provisions.

Black Comedy was tall, so Jill was able to keep back and follow without getting too close. In some places, she could see over the hedges and keep Ruby and Rapide in sight. They trotted for at least seven miles until they turned down a small road where Jill had never been before. After ten minutes, they came to Cranley Common.

It was an overgrown village, littered with bungalows, each with a concrete path and a small, uninspiring patch of grass. A neat gate marked the entry to each of these small houses, the haven of small people without large ambitions but proud of their own homes.

Beyond the village, the road wound upwards through a wood and came out on a bare hillside. It was not the magnificent rolling downs that can be found in other areas of England, but rather a series of small hills intersected with wire fences and scattered with smallholdings. It was a field away from a main road with petrol stations and ramshackle cafes. In the distance, one could see Bottom New Town.

Jill was finding it hard to keep Ruby in view without showing herself. She had turned off from the road down a lane. Rapide was trotting along a ragged grass verge at a fair clip. Perhaps he knew that his best chum, Black Boy, would be somewhere along this rutted lane. Jill hung back. She pulled up Black Comedy and got out the binoculars. Ruby rode straight into the yard at the side of the house at the end of the lane, which was a dead end. Throwing herself out of the saddle, she hooked Rapide's reins over a post. Perhaps she was planning to steal Rapide as well, and this was her contact. It was hard to believe that the young girl should be so ruthless, but it was possible that she was under the control of a conniving criminal, perhaps a relative, and she was doing it to help her mother, who was poverty-stricken and chronically ill. Or perhaps she just didn't want Black Boy to go to the Bullhorns and was determined to save him. However, it was hard to figure out what would be her long-term plan. Would she attempt to keep Black Boy hidden forever? Was Lavender in on this? Ruby didn't seem like the sort of person who would steal her best friend's favourite pony. Following Ruby to this unprepossessing place was posing more questions, not providing any answers.

The wind was blowing towards her, and Jill could hear voices. Ruby's shrill high tones and a male voice. They seemed to be exchanging sharp words. Jill trained the binoculars on the yard, but she could only see Rapide tied to the gate. Black Comedy was restless. He sensed Jill's disquiet, and he didn't like it. They had come a long way, at least fifteen miles. It was territory that Jill had never been to.

Finally, she saw Ruby come running out of the yard, her arms waving like flags. She unhooked Rapide's reins and scrambled into the saddle. A sallow man, as long and thin as a runner bean, was walking towards her shaking his fist. A white bull terrier was yapping at her heels. Ruby spun Rapide around and kicked him into a wild canter, and they escaped back down the lane. Jill sat there and waited for her. It was time for an explanation, and she was determined to get the truth out of Ruby. She positioned Black Comedy across the narrow lane, blocking Ruby and Rapide's passage.

"Get outta way!" shouted Ruby, "I gotta get away!"

Then she recognised Jill and Black Comedy.

"Is you!" she said. "You caught me!"

"It would appear so," replied Jill, determined to keep her cool.

"Come on, we gotta go," said Ruby, trying to push Black Boy past Black Comedy.

"You have to tell me what is happening, or I am going straight to the police," said Jill in a dark, threatening voice.

"Is not wot was meant to 'appen," said Ruby. Tears were streaming down her face.

"It's Black Boy, isn't it? You took him," said Jill.

Ruby nodded her head.

"'e is me uncle. Well, kinda uncle, more a cousin, second cousin. I ask'd 'im to look after Black Boy til I couldda work out wot to do and now 'e's gone and sold 'im. 'e won't tell me where, or anyfing. Wot are we gonna do?"

"What we are going to do is turn around, and I will talk to him. If he doesn't tell me, then we will call the police. He is receiving stolen goods," said Jill with quiet determination. "Don't worry, we won't dismount; if it comes to it, we can gallop away."

"But if the cops get innit then I'm a thief, and they'll sen' me to one of them 'omes," said Ruby in despair.

"Well, let's hope it doesn't come to that," said Jill grimly. She braced her shoulders and arranged her face in a determined expression.

She rode down the lane, and Ruby followed extremely unwillingly. The closer Jill got to the establishment, the more she realised its cheerless aspect. It was a gimcrack bungalow that looked unfinished as if the builder had given up before completion. Beyond its wire-fenced boundary were an old gravel pit, a railway line and a clutch of dismal allotments with broken-down old sheds and overgrown vegetable plots in the middle distance. A couple of scrawny chickens were scratching fruitlessly in the yard, and there was no sign of the unsavoury relative. One of the window panes was missing and had been patched with a square of cardboard.

"Hello, is anyone here!" shouted Jill. She was furious and felt strong and relentless, but there was an edge of nervous fear in her. She wondered if she shouldn't go straight to the police rather than try and investigate this for herself. Ruby was sitting on Rapide near the entrance of the yard as if poised to gallop away when there was trouble.

The man Jill had seen through the binoculars appeared. Up close, he was even more unsavoury. He grimaced at her revealing a set of horribly neglected teeth stained yellow from nicotine.

"Wotcha want?" he asked belligerently, shooting a murderous glance at Ruby.

"It's about the black pony that Ruby brought here two nights ago. Where is he? I want to take him back to his owners."

"I doan know what she be tellin' you, but it's all lies. I ain't had no black pony 'ere," he replied aggressively.

"Please be reasonable," said Jill with as much authority as she could put into her voice. "I won't go to the police if you tell us now where we can locate the pony."

"It be the coppers involved that little varmint is the one who should be charged," said the unpleasant man.

"Well, let's avoid the police. We just want to get the pony back," said Jill reasonably.

The man looked cunning at this point.

"You want information, you pay," he said sharply.

"In that case, it is the police, and Ruby will take her chances," said Jill.

"Get orf me property!" shouted the man.

Reluctantly Jill turned Black Comedy round and rode away. Ruby followed, looking crestfallen and despairing.

"What do we do now?" asked Jill. "I can't think of any solution but the police. You'll have to come clean, Ruby."

"It'll be my word against his," said Ruby, thinking quickly, "and we still won't get Black Boy back."

"What did he tell you he'd done with Black Boy?" asked Jill.

"'e said he was too much to feed, and he sold 'im on, but 'e didn't say to who," replied Ruby miserably.

"Perhaps the Bullhorns would have been preferable to this," replied Jill acerbically.

They rode in silence for ten minutes.

"Do you know anyone who is acquainted with that man or a relative who might be able to give us more information?" asked Jill. "What is his name anyway?"

"'e's Billy Dudgeon. 'e's got loads of contacts. But there's my Aunty Nora. She might know 'ow to get 'im to tell the truth. She's scary, and most of the family is afraid of 'er."

"Aunty Nora," said Jill. "Where does she live?"

"She's another five miles on, in Bottom New Town."

"What an unfortunate name," remarked Jill. "I think we had better take these horses home and borrow a car and continue to investigate. Perhaps we can get Henry and Ann to drive us, and they can be back up. Come on, let's get going before poor Black Boy gets shipped over to France and ends up as dinner."

"They eat 'orsemeat over there," said Ruby, aghast.

"Yes, they do," replied Jill grimly.

They got back to the Ellison-Heaths and put Rapide in the field with Summer Fancy, who whinnied with relief to have his new friend as company. There was no one around and no time to seek out Lavender or her parents and explain what had happened. For this, Ruby was grateful. If only they could rescue Black Boy before she had to explain what she had done.

Ruby jumped up behind Black Comedy's saddle and bumped around as Jill pushed him into a canter all the way back to Pool Cottage. Black Comedy was not a comfortable ride at the best of times, and Ruby was hanging on for grim death, her arms wrapped around Jill's waist.

"Thank goodness, Ann and Henry are here!" exclaimed Jill as they careered up the driveway and clattered into the stable yard.

"Quick, Ruby! You unsaddle Black Comedy and put him in a loose box. Make sure he has hay and water and I'll go and tell them what is happening."

Jill found Ann and Henry sitting at the kitchen table having a late lunch.

"Just in time, Jill! You must try my new creation. It's a jelly and banana tart!" crowed Ann.

"How can you think of food when Black Boy's been stolen?" demanded Jill. "I've found out where he was taken, but now he's gone. We've got to take action before the trail goes cold."

Ann and Henry stared at her in astonishment.

"Have the police found something out?" asked Henry.

"No, I've been playing detective, and I followed Ruby, and it was her who took him to some ghastly ill-bred man called Billy Dudgeon, but he's sold him on, and we've got to investigate."

"Surely, it's up to the plods," said Henry.

"There's no time. If we don't succeed, then we will report it, but if we can possibly avoid it, I'd like to keep Ruby out of it," explained Jill.

"So, what should we do?" asked Ann, getting up and pulling on her coat.

"There's another relative that is some sort of matriarch in Ruby's extended family, her Aunt Nora in Bottom New Town. Apparently, she holds some sway and might get Billy to tell where he sold Black Boy."

"Bottom New Town!" exclaimed Henry. "That's a rough place!"

"I'm sure the three of us will cope with a visit to the wrong end of Oxfordshire!" snapped Jill.

Ruby rushed in.

"You took Black Boy," said Henry sternly.

"This is no time for recriminations, Henry," said Ann firmly. "We can deal with the rights and wrongs of it later. Now we have to take action."

They rushed in a body out to Henry's Land Rover. Jill and Ruby got in the back, and Ann sat in the passenger seat.

"First, I want to go to this man's place. Perhaps with more of us, he might come clean," said Henry. "After that, we'll go to Bottom New Town. Directions, please!"

Ruby directed him down along the main road and then into a maze of rutted roads that wound through the hills, going deep into poor man's land.

"I've never been this way before," said Ann, gazing out of the window with interest. "I had no idea there were all these smallholdings nearby."

"You've obviously had a sheltered life," said Henry. "Paris and Switzerland but you don't know what's at the other end of the county."

They bumped down the rutted lane to Billy Dudgeon's house and parked in the yard.

"Anyone home!" shouted Henry in a deep voice. Jill and Ann scrambled out and began to poke around the yard, looking for clues. Ruby cowered in the back of the Land Rover, too afraid and ashamed to get out.

"You can see there's been a pony shut up in this tool shed," said Ann. "Look horse manure! And it's relatively fresh."

"And hoof prints!" said Jill looking at the imprints in a puddle near the shed door.

Henry was banging on the back door.

"There's obviously no one home. He must have scarpered in case the police turned up," he said, trying the door handle, but it was locked.

"I've never known anyone live with a window blocked up by cardboard," said Ann thoughtfully. "Do you think Ruby could squeeze through there and let us in?"

"Isn't that breaking and entering?" said Henry reprovingly.

"Not really. It's her relative, and we're not actually breaking but removing some tatty cardboard," said Jill. "Ruby! Ruby! Come here! You've got to wriggle in here and let us in so we can see if there are any clues inside."

Ruby climbed out the back of the Land Rover.

"Lucky I'm so small," she said.

"A regular little Oliver Twist!" joked Ann, "that makes us Fagan."

"Forget the literary allusions," said Jill. "Come on, hurry up. We're running out of time. That horrible man might come back."

Ruby slid through the window pane and opened the back door, and the others trooped in.

"What are we looking for?" asked Henry.

"Some sort of clue. A name, a phone number, anything that might tell us where he sent the pony," said Jill.

The inside of the house was worse than the outside. Grime coated every surface. It wasn't just dust but grease and dirt. A pile of smelly clothes was thrown in one corner of the kitchen.

"Henry, you look through those pockets. Men's dirty underpants are just not suitable for females such as ourselves," said Ann, who even in such dramatic circumstances was still witty, retaining her sense of humour.

"This is much worse than pulling a calf out of a cow having trouble birthing," said Henry wrinkling his nose.

Ann and Jill were scurrying through some half-open drawers from which spilt every type of household detritus.

"There are some phone numbers written on this bit of paper," said Henry, waving a dirty scrap triumphantly in the air.

"Brill!" said Ann. "If they're in his pockets, there's a chance they've been used recently."

"Have you come up with anything else?" asked Henry. "I'm not feeling comfortable here. I could be struck off as a vet for this escapade!"

"There's nothing here that seems of any use," said Jill. "I guess we've got to hope that those phone numbers will lead us on the trail."

"Let's go then," said Henry. "I don't feel in the mood for confronting this Billy character. I'm no John Wayne!"

"You're my hero!" said Ann, giving him an admiring smile.

They piled back into the old Land Rover and jolted down the track at a much faster speed than that which Henry usually drove. Jill and Ruby were rattling around in the back, bouncing off their seats and hitting their heads on the roof.

"Back to Pool Cottage, and we'll hit the phones!" shouted Ann.

Jill wondered if Ann wasn't enjoying this adventure a bit too much. She was stricken with fear for what might have happened to Black Boy. Ruby was unnaturally silent, her face tear-stained, her expression woebegone.

"I know you meant it for the best," said Jill quietly to her. "But you didn't have a plan."

"Outta the frying pan in the fire," whispered Ruby.

They dashed back into Pool Cottage. Ann went straight to the phone and dialled the first number. Her exuberant mood drained out of her as the number was answered.

"Can you give me your address?" she asked. "We want to drop off some stock." She wrote down an address.

"What is it?" asked Jill, snatching up the notes Ann had made.

"It's the slaughterhouse at Bottom New Town," said Ann, her face as white as if it had been dipped in chalk dust.

"Oh no! Oh no!" cried Jill.

Ruby was swamped with fear and guilt. She had caused this with her impetuous, well-meaning actions. She had put Black Boy in grave danger, and perhaps he would be killed and served up for dinner across the Channel.

"We must go there straight away!" cried Ann. "Come on, Henry! We must save him!"

"We don't know for sure that he has gone there," said Henry. "I think we should call the police and ask them to help us. The knackery isn't going to hand him over on our say-so. We have to think this through. It's no good getting in a flap."

"There's no time! We must go immediately. We can ring the police once we're there," argued Ann.

"No, I will ring the police now, and then we'll go. They'll have finished the killing for today anyway," insisted Henry.

"The killing!" cried Jill, tears welling in her eyes. It took a lot for Jill to cry, as readers would know. It was not a common occurrence.

Henry seemed to take ages on the phone to the police. He talked to at least three individuals before he got on to someone who seemed to grasp the situation. The three girls were in agony waiting for him to get off the phone. They wailed and gnashed their teeth. When he hung up, he suggested that they let the Ellison-Heaths know what was happening. Ruby was twisting and turning in despair. She was sure now that her behaviour was going to become known. Nothing could protect her. She would lose Lavender as a friend forever. Her job as the girl groom at the Ellison-Heaths. Mrs Darcy, Wendy and Serena would not let her near the riding school. She had destroyed her life with a single night's impetuous action.

"Henry, darling, we can talk to them later if we actually find him. Do come on!" cried Ann.

They piled into the Land Rover and set off for Bottom New Town. Henry knew the way as occasionally he was called to visit the knackery when their regular vet was away. They drove up as the workers were leaving — unattractive men who smelt of blood and gore, with greasy hair and murderous glints in their eyes.

"I'll go in by myself," said Henry. "Histrionics and passionate pleas are not going to help this situation."

Ann and Jill looked at each other. Perhaps he was right. He strode up to the office and went in to talk to the manager. Jill was wringing her hands in despair. She should never have sold Black Boy and Rapide. It had been the worst mistake of her life. How could she have betrayed them in this way?

It seemed like an age, but eventually, Henry emerged. He looked worried.

"They've had a couple of ponies go through the works today. One was black, but we don't know for sure that it was Black Boy. The manager looked up the records, and he seemed bigger, perhaps 14.2 hh, but we're not sure how accurate that is."

Jill couldn't breathe. A black suffocating cloud of despair enveloped her. Ruby felt sick. She slid out the back door of the Land Rover and retched into the muddy grass.

"The police rang the manager while I was in there, and any other black ponies turn up, they'll hold them back and wait for some identification," went on Henry.

"Is there any way of . . . looking at the remains? Perhaps I could identify him?" whispered Jill.

"That's an idea," said Henry. "Come back with me, and we'll find out what they do with the hides."

"This is too ghastly for words. Jill, can you bear to look at that? Surely it will be too gruesome," said Ann.

"We have to know," replied Jill grimly.

It seemed like an age before Henry and Jill walked back out.

"No white star," said Henry. "It's not Black Boy!"

Ann was ready to pass out with relief. Ruby couldn't quite recover herself. Slowly they drove back to Pool Cottage. Henry made them all cups of strong tea, heaped with sugar and toast piled with butter and jam.

"You all need to eat. Pull yourselves together," he instructed. "Now we need to try those other phone numbers. Perhaps they will lead us to Black Boy."

"Take heart, comrades!" said Ann, drawing strength from Henry's practical resolve. "It wasn't Black Boy. It could have been, but it wasn't. Give me those pieces of paper. I'm going to get on the blower."

"The blower," echoed Jill faintly.

Ann dialled another number on the list. She stood poised over a telephone pad with a pencil, ready to make notes. It rang and rang, and she was about to give up when it was answered.

"Oh! Hello!" she said, trying to moderate her middle-class accent to match the voice on the other end of the line. "I'm trying to find a pony to buy, an animal suitable for my little girl. I was given your number by a chap in a pub. Do you know where I might find a good pony?"

She grimaced to the others, well aware of how weird this might sound if it were a person who had nothing to do with horses.

"Who gave you me number?" barked the voice suspiciously.

"I think his name was Billy. Yes, he said his name was Billy."

"Billy was after sellin' me a pony, but it was dodgy, so I told him to take a runner. Don't ring 'ere agin."

The phone cut off.

"Billy tried to sell him a pony, but he says he said no," said Ann.

"Do you think he was telling the truth or just denying it. Maybe he did buy Black Boy?" suggested Jill hesitantly.

"Can we find an address through a phone number?" asked Ann.

"No, but the police can. We may just have to give them this list of numbers. Ruby is going to have to admit to what she did," replied Henry.

"How many more numbers are there?" asked Ann. "Perhaps I should take a different tack and find out where they live before I mention a stolen pony. Any ideas what type of story I might spin?"

"There's two more. I can't think how you might get their addresses. If someone I didn't know rang up and asked me my address, I would be suspicious," said Henry frowning.

The four of them sat in silence, each thinking intently.

"We could tell 'em they've won a prize, and we need an address to send it," suggested Ruby. "I know it's not true, but."

"We could send them a prize, then it would be true," said Ann. "Something inexpensive but a prize all the same. If they ask what the prize is, we could say it is a mystery. People love the idea of getting something for nothing."

"Alright, that sounds good to me," said Jill, "we've got to do something, and if it doesn't work, we'll go to the police."

"Here goes! said Ann.

She dialled the number and waited. It was picked up within two rings.

"Good evening," she began in a pleasant voice. "To whom do I have the pleasure of speaking?"

"Mr Cutler, this is Miss Derry. I have great pleasure in telling you that you have won a mystery prize in our current competition."

She waited for a moment.

"Yes, congratulations. Now, if you would like to give me your address, I will arrange despatch through the postal system first thing tomorrow morning."

"Yes, yes . . . good-bye and congratulations again."

She turned to the others. "Now *that* ruse worked."

"What is the address?" asked Jill.

"It's Cranley Common. That dreary little place that I rode through this morning following Ruby," said Jill. "This morning seems like aeons ago."

"Let's do the other one before we set off," said Ann. "I don't suppose it's worth ringing that first number and trying the mystery prize on them?"

"They might be suspicious," said Jill. "We'll do the other number, and then we'll go and snoop and see if we can spot Black Boy. If that doesn't work, then we'll go to the police."

"Agreed," said Henry.

The next phone call also worked like a charm, and they had another address, this one on the far side of Birtle.

"Let's go to Cranley Common first," said Jill. "I have a feeling that's where he is."

"You and your feelings," said Ann laughing, light-heartedly. At least they had something to act on.

They piled back into the Land Rover. It was dark now.

"Hang on!" said Henry. "Flashlights! If we're to snoop around in the dark looking for a black pony, we're going to need some light."

Ann dashed back to the stable yard and found the two torches that they kept on the shelf in the tack room.

"Let's go baby-o!" she called. Henry did a three-point turn and they roared out onto the road.

"Tally-ho!" shouted Jill.

Chapter Twenty – Hot on the Trail

They sped back to Cranley Common. Ann was reading Henry's map to find 15 Cherry Tree Lane. They turned into the street, and reading the numbers on the gates, they came to number 15.

"Surely you couldn't keep a pony in one of these tiny back gardens," said Ann. "If this person did buy Black Boy then they must keep him somewhere else. Is there a local riding school nearby?"

"Would there be a field aroun' the back, behind the house mebbe? suggested Ruby.

"Perhaps," said Ann. "Ruby, you and I can creep around the back. Perhaps Jill and Henry could pretend to be doing, . . . I know a survey. A survey about pets, and in it a question about a pony, that should work."

"Hang on," said Jill. "If the survey works, then you don't need to go creeping around the back. What if you got caught? Then we could all be in deep trouble."

"But I would rather enjoy snooping around like we were working for the resistance of something," replied Ann flippantly.

"This isn't a joke. This is Black Boy!" cried Jill, tears glistening in her eyes.

"We're all getting overwrought. Now calm down. Jill is right. There's no need to go sneaking around and trespassing. Let's try the survey first," said Henry.

"If you're going to do a survey, then you've got to at least have a clipboard and perhaps some questions on it. To make it look official," said Ann.

"I've got a clipboard here and some forms that I use to record information about cows. As long as they don't get a good look at them, they're not going to know," said Henry.

Henry and Jill climbed out of the Land Rover, let themselves in through the small gate and marched up to the front door.

Ann and Ruby sat in the car watching. A woman opened the door and stood illuminated in the doorway. It seemed to take some persuasion on the part of Henry before she let them into the house. The front door was shut.

"Wot if I jus' slip out and take a gander roun' the back?" suggested Ruby.

"I want to say yes, but if you get caught, and they don't have a pony, then that would be a lot of explaining to do. And we've already got a lot of explaining to do. So, no."

It seemed an age before Henry and Jill emerged from the house.

"Well? Well?" demanded Ann.

"No pony," said Henry, "but a rather interesting collection of dogs, cat, goldfish and even a lizard."

"Oh," said Ann, crestfallen. "I wonder why their phone number was in Billy's pocket."

"I have no idea," said Henry. "I certainly wasn't going to ask them."

"Let's go on to the address in Birtle. It's getting late and knocking on someone's door late in the evening is going to be a bit weird," said Jill, looking pale but determined.

At Birtle, they had more luck. This time Ann went with Henry. Jill and Ruby waited in the Land Rover. In the gathering dusk, they could see a field beside the house. It was only a tiny cottage, and the field was small, and there didn't seem much grazing. Ruby darted out and scouted around and then came back.

"There's fresh manure," she said, "but no pony."

"Perhaps this is it," said Jill.

Eventually, Henry and Ann came out. They waved to Jill and Ruby, and they jumped out of the Land Rover and ran up.

"I think we've found him," said Ann breathlessly. "But it's tragic. That little girl adores him, and her parents have been saving forever to buy him. They think they've got this absolute bargain because he was so cheap."

"He's stolen!" burst out Jill in outraged accents.

"I know, Jill," said Ann soothingly, but the little girl, Clarabell, doesn't know that!"

"Clarabell!" snorted Jill. "Sounds like a cow!"

"Come back in and meet them and I'm sure that will soften your heart," said Ann, realising just how stressed was Jill.

Jill stalked ahead of them to the front door. Her heart was hardened. She wanted Black Boy back, sent to Scotland, where he would be safe, and this could never happen again.

The family inside were sitting huddled together in front of a very small gas fire. They looked like they were about to be dragged off by the Gestapo.

"Mr Thurston has explained that we've bought Black Boy from someone who had no right to sell him," said the father, a wispy man with watery blue eyes and hair that was retreating backwards over his scalp at a rate of knots.

"Oh, we had no idea," said his wife, wringing her hands in distress.

"I love him so much, my little Blackie," said the young girl who must be Clarabell.

"That Billy Dudgeon had no right to sell him!" retorted Jill.

"Look," said Henry in a quiet, reasonable voice. "This is most unfortunate, but first we want to see him, just to make sure that he really is Black Boy."

"He's out the back. We've put him in the potting shed," said the father.

"The potting shed!" exploded Jill.

"Jill, you seem to forget that we've not all got every facility," said Ann, who had never felt the need to speak to Jill like this before.

"I'll show him to you," said Clarabell, drawing herself up to her full height, which was not tall. She led the way through a tiny kitchen and out the back door. The potting shed was at the end of the garden.

"We let him out in the field beside the house during the day. I've done everything I could to make him comfortable at night."

It was Black Boy who seemed to be surprised to be disturbed during his evening snooze. However, he did look contented and loved. He was well-groomed and had a bed of thick straw and just enough room to lie down if he chose. The water bucket was scrubbed and filled with clean water, and he had a well-stuffed hay net hanging on the wall.

"Oh! Black Boy! It was all my fault! I should never, never, have sold you!" cried Jill, burying her head in his mane, her arms clasped around his neck.

Clarabell stood by the door looking utterly woebegone. Her parents were grey with worry, thinking they had been receiving stolen goods and might be sent to prison for years.

"We know that you didn't know that he was stolen," said Ann gently, trying to make up for Jill's harsh attitude.

"We don't want to involve the police if this can be solved. I think the key is to approach Billy Dudgeon and ask him for your money back, and then Black Boy can be returned to the Ellison-Heaths," said Henry.

"Perhaps if we can get our money back, we could buy him off the real owners," said the father bravely.

"Oh yes!" cried the little Clarabell hopefully.

"No!" said Jill, "I want him back!"

"Well, first we need to go back to Billy Dudgeon and see if he will return the money. We'll threaten him with the police. Then, we have to talk to the Ellison-Heaths and see if we can come up with a solution. I think that Mr Street and I should go alone to Billy Dudgeon's. We don't want him confronted with a crowd of distressed females," continued Henry.

At this point, Ann, who had distinct feminist tendencies, could have objected, but she was worried about Jill.

Mrs Street, Clarabell, Jill, Ann and Ruby crowded back into the tiny living room, and there wasn't enough room for them to sit down. Jill stood with her back against the wall, her arms folded defensively, a grim expression on her face. Clarabell was collapsed on a rug, curled up in a ball of distress and helplessness. Ruby was worried. She was very aware that she had caused this appalling situation.

"I want to buy him off the Ellison-Heaths and send him to Scotland. We've set up the stables now as a riding school, and he has done that sort of work before. At least then he'll be safe," said Jill glaring balefully at Ruby, who hung her head and shuffled her feet.

Ann was worried. She felt sorry for little Clarabell, who obviously adored Black Boy. She understood Jill's feelings but hoped that her best friend's heart might be softened once she calmed down.

"What if you bought him and lent him to Clarabell until she grows out of him, and then he could go to Scotland to live in splendid retirement," she suggested in a reasonable voice.

It was then that Ruby realised that whatever happened, she was never going to have Black Boy to ride every day ever again. In fact, after this escapade, she would be lucky if the Ellison-Heaths would ever talk to her again. There was still no certainty that she would not be arrested by the police.

Time stretched on. It was two hours since Henry and Mr Street had left and was now ten o'clock at night.

"Won't your mother be worried, Ruby?" asked Ann.

"She prob'ly won't notice," replied the young girl.

Jill looked at her. She couldn't imagine her mother not noticing if she hadn't returned home at ten at night when she was twelve years old, or even fifteen or sixteen. She caught a glimpse of what it must be like to be a child of a family like Ruby's. This moment of insight was followed by a rush of compassion for Clarabell. She remembered how she had longed for a pony and how much she had loved Black Boy when she had first got him. They had been poor, and she had struggled. If it hadn't been for Martin Lowe and his kindness and help, she might never have become a competent horsewoman.

Eventually, Henry and Mr Street returned. They looked exhausted as if they had been tussling with the devil himself.

"We got the money back, but Billy is not happy. I don't think you want to be visiting that relative in the near future, Ruby."

"Me family is goan never fergiv me," said Ruby quietly.

"I want to take Black Boy now," insisted Jill.

"Please, no, just one more night," begged Clarabell.

"Absolutely not," retorted Jill. She couldn't bear for Black Boy to disappear again.

Henry agreed that Jill was to stay at the Streets', and he would go and get the horse trailer, and they would take him back to Pool Cottage that very night. Mrs Street put Clarabell to bed. Ruby was dropped off at Ditching Hollow and Ann was to prepare some supper for Henry and Jill when they returned. After all the excitement they were totally drained and needed some sustenance.

Now that Black Boy was safely back in Chatton, Ann turned her mind to Jill. She was perplexed by the way that her best friend was behaving. This was not the common sense, jolly and essentially well-meaning Jill. There was something wrong with her friend and she was determined to get to the bottom of it.

She knew about the financial problems at Blainstock Castle and the ambitious project to make the stables pay. She didn't think this was the real issue for Jill, who had not always been rich and was resourceful and practical when it came to making ends meet. Perhaps it was related to going to Australia? Although on the face of it, such a trip promised to be tremendous fun and an exciting experience. Somehow, Jill didn't seem to be looking forward to it. It was ridiculous, but she sensed that Jill was afraid. She was going to have to sit her down, just the two of them and one way or another, get the truth out of her.

The situation with Black Boy was resolved. The Ellison-Heaths agreed to sell him to Jill, and he could remain at Pool Cottage for a few months until Jill returned from Australia and could take him to Scotland. The dreaded Bullhorns had been informed that he had been sold to someone else. Ann had lent Jill the money for his purchase which was considerably more than he was worth, but no one cared.

Mr and Mrs Ellison-Heath received no satisfactory explanation for Black Boy's disappearance. The police had always suspected that it was an insurance fraud and were happy to be told that he had been found. Susan King and Porsche's plot to sell him to the Bullhorns was thwarted, but Susan was more interested in pursuing her dalliance with Austin, and Porsche was now down to only one horse since Mangala had been put down.

Lavender knew that it had been Ruby, and she wasn't sure what to think. Black Boy had been in more danger in the hands of Ruby's dubious relatives than he might have been with the Bullhorns. She had to face the fact that one way or the other, she had lost him, and her heart was broken.

There was only one day left before Jill had to leave to fly to Australia. She and Ann had a cosy supper together in front of the glowing fire in the living room of Pool Cottage.

"Jill, darling, will you answer a question honestly?" began Ann.

"I'm always honest," retorted Jill as if her integrity was being questioned.

"What is it about this trip to Australia that has twisted you up?" asked Ann, staring straight into Jill's eyes with a laser glance.

Sometimes Ann's questions dropped onto the listener with the approximate weight and impact of a falling piano, and this time she might have dropped a bomb.

Jill began to sob.

"My darling, Jillikins!" exclaimed Ann. This was obviously serious. "Tell me all. Can it be that bad? What on earth is it?" she asked. "You must trust me to tell me, Jill. A trouble shared and all that."

"You have no idea!" cried Jill melodramatically, tears streaming down her face. "My whole life, I believed something, and it wasn't true!"

"Tell!" demanded Ann. "You have to tell me!"

"Promise you won't let on to a soul, not even Henry!" said Jill, her voice dropping to a whisper. "Mummy told me just before I left. I had absolutely no idea. It has been cartwheeling through my mind, like an endless reel, and then Black Boy going missing. It was as if everything that I believed in my childhood was being wrenched away from me."

"Are you adopted?" asked Ann, hazarding a guess.

"Not exactly. Mummy is my mother, but my father isn't dead!" announced Jill.

"What!" gasped Ann, dropping her solicitous manner like a hot brick. She was shocked to the core. "But where is he?"

"In Australia."

For once, Ann was silenced. Her mouth hung open like a goldfish in mid-gulp.

"I was always told that he went away on a business trip and died. There was never much detail, and somehow I hadn't wanted to know. I wasn't at all curious. I just accepted it because that was the way it had always been."

"Why on earth would your mother tell everyone he was dead. Did he run away with a floozy, and she couldn't bear the whispering behind her back?" asked Ann.

"He went to prison," said Jill in a whisper. "The shame of it would have killed Mummy, everyone pointing at her, the wife of a murderer, and I would have been the child of a murderer. They would have said that it was in my blood."

Who did he murder?" asked Ann.

"Well, no one, or so Mummy says, but perhaps it's not true, perhaps he really was a murderer, but she said it was a tragic mistake and it was only by the hugest good luck that he didn't hang. It was an accident, but it looked like he'd done it deliberately."

"How long was he in prison?"

"He was released when I was eighteen, and he jumped on a ship and went to Australia. He didn't even meet up with Mummy. By then, they had been divorced for years, and with Richard on the scene, it was too difficult. She showed me a letter he had sent."

"Didn't he want to meet you?" asked Ann, "his long lost child."

"He did, but then Mummy said it was going to be hard enough for me to adjust to her and Richard, and moving to Scotland, and everything and she begged him to leave things the way they had been for so long."

"I've got about a million questions racing through my mind," said Ann. "Your poor mother. I suppose there was no one she could trust. Does Richard know?"

"Mummy deals with it herself. But that's not the point. I've got a father, an actual real, living, breathing father, and I have no idea what I am meant to think, let alone what I'm meant to feel," said Jill.

"Who did he kill?" asked Ann, her mind shifting to the macabre and wanting the gory details.

"He didn't kill them. It was an accident. It was his cheating business partner, anyway," cried Jill, thinking that if this was Ann's reaction, she could understand how Mummy hadn't wanted them to bear the burden of public knowledge all these years. "Mummy didn't give me the details. If I meet up with him, I guess I could ask. Although I'm not sure that that would be very polite."

"I think politeness is the last issue," exclaimed Ann.

"He is living in what they call the Snowy Mountains," said Jill, "and we are going near that area in our tour of the East Coast, so I guess I will be able to go off and meet him."

"Gosh! That will be weird!" said Ann. "I wonder if you look like him?"

Jill was a little impatient with Ann's prevarications, a perverse interest in what was inconsequential. Who did he kill? What did he look like? That wasn't the point. The fact was that she had a father and that single overwhelming fact had swept through her being and mentally knocked her off her feet.

"Jill, please, please write and tell me what happens in Australia," begged Ann.

"Are you just thinking this is a fascinating story and not really caring about me?" asked Jill.

"Oh! Jillikins! Of course not. You know I care about you. It's just such a fantastic story, and it was there all the time, and we didn't have a clue," said Ann. "Is this going to go in your Jill stories?"

The thought of letting the whole world know about such a personal thing was abhorrent to Jill.

"It would be a marvellous plot twist," went on Ann. "You know, like all those stories of long-lost fathers. You might even have a half-sibling! Although, you already have little Hamish, a half-brother."

"Stop it! Stop it!" shouted Jill. "I suppose I will write and tell you, but you must read my letters and then burn them. This is absolutely top secret, and you can't even tell one single person."

The conversation went on long into the night. Jill found herself standing back a little and viewing the matter with some perspective, almost as if it were happening to someone else, but not quite. It did help to talk to Ann. She did trust Ann, who had been her faithful best friend for so many years.

They eventually went to bed and slept late. The next morning, with one day left in Chatton, Jill wanted to go to Mrs Darcy's and see her friends. She wanted to be in a place where she felt safe. Mrs Darcy wasn't there. She was off visiting in the neighbourhood. Wendy was busy in the office, and Serena was leaving to go and ride Patchwork.

"Would you like to come with me?" she asked.

"You could see you step-relative, Mark," said Ann with an impish grin.

"Why not?" said Jill, who was still in a strange mood.

They followed Serena in her car and pulled up to the Farthingtons. Jill wondered how they had never got to know these eccentric old ladies when they had been children. The house was like something out of a storybook, so old, tumbledown and romantic.

They went inside, calling out their arrival, and Serena took them to the dining room. Jill did smile at the sight of Mark Lansdowne beavering away, cleaning soiled hay off the wooden floor beneath the crystal chandelier.

"Hello Mark," she couldn't resist. "It seems our paths are to cross again."

Mark looked up and glowered at the sight of them. He didn't reply and turned his back and continued to fork bedding into the wheelbarrow.

"This is Patchwork," said Serena, who was unaware of Jill's relationship with Mark. "Isn't he just gorgeous? You know Mark rode him to victory at the Tiddington Hunter Trials in the novice event. "You're such a good, clever boy," she said, rubbing his ears gently.

"Mark or Patchwork?" asked Jill sarkily.

Serena looked at her in surprise. She didn't understand Jill's attitude at all.

"I'll saddle him up, and we can do some schooling in the paddock. You could have a ride if you like," she said, a little hesitantly.

"No, no," said Ann. "You show us his paces. We'll watch."

They left Mark to his manual labour.

"He must be stuck on Mercedes to submit to this situation," said Jill wonderingly. "Do you think she is interested in him?"

"Well, by all accounts, they're just about an item," said Ann. "It does seem to have brought out the best in Mark. He has to play-act a decent person, and perhaps it will turn him into a good person. I imagine the prize of marrying Mercedes is a pretty big incentive."

"It is all a bit close to home," said Jill. "I never imagined that Mark would live in Chatton or at least Shrove Langton. It doesn't sit well with me."

"I suppose he didn't like you going to Scotland," said Ann in a reasonable tone. "Anyway, they might set up a yard anywhere in England. They won't necessarily stay at Pevensy Park."

"I would have rather he'd married that ghastly Diana Barton-Tompkin and disappeared into the depths of Yorkshire, never to be seen again," said Jill.

"Life winds us around some mysterious paths," said Ann philosophically.

"Doesn't it just," remarked Jill ruefully.

The next morning, Ann took Jill to the railway station to go to London.

"I've just had a thought!" cried Ann. "The Cannon twins! Norrie and Dorrie! You can get n touch with them in Australia. I'll write to them, I've got their parents' address and give them the address at the Heywards."

Jill and Ann had met these girls while they were messing around doing pony jobs after they had left school. They were Australian riding champions. The train slid to a hissing stop and Ann helped Jill with her luggage as she climbed aboard.

"Have fun!" shouted Ann.

"I'll try," said Jill bravely. She leaned out the window waving until the train chugged around the corner.

Then, Ann drove to Mrs Darcy's. She had an idea that she thought might help sweet little Clarabell. Now that Black Boy would be company for Black Comedy, she thought it might be possible to move Totty, the little retired pony to Clarabell's. The girl was only eight years old and small for her age, so it wouldn't hurt if she rode Totty around the lanes a little and she could lavish all her love and attention on the old gelding, who had served so long and faithfully at the riding school.

Mrs Darcy agreed to the plan on the condition that Ann regularly visited to make sure that Clarabell wasn't riding poor Totty to death and that he was being fed correctly. Ann was delighted. She liked it when everything turned out well, especially when she had masterminded events. Clarabell had a pony to love. Black Boy was safe at Pool Cottage. Lavender would have to learn to love Summer Fancy, who, although being a push-button show pony, was still possessed of a pony soul and needed love like every other kind of pony. She was sure that Jill would have a smashing time in Australia and hopefully would find her father a decent chap and come to terms with that situation. Now, Ann had to set her mind to tell Henry that she had decided not to go to Bristol, and then he would propose. They could be married in June, and Jill would be back for the wedding. All would be right with the world.

THE END